"Tessa, come on. Lie down."

Only a moment ago she'd been holding it together just fine, and then Reilly had to bring that long, sleekly muscled body of his close. Didn't he know what that magnificent near nudity did to a woman?

Tessa shook her head, not sure whether she was refusing his command or trying to rid herself of the images his husky voice brought to mind. Images of hot summer nights, satin sheets and wild, sweet lovemaking...

Reilly took matters into his own hands. He led her to the cot and helped her sit. "Just lie down, right here."

His head was bent close to hers...his lips definitely within kissing distance. The room shrank in size until it was just about the two of them, their breaths mingling.

"So, tell me, Reilly." She licked her suddenly dry lips. "If I lie down, do I get a good-night kiss?"

Dear Reader,

It's Harlequin Temptation's twentieth birthday and we're ready to do some celebrating. After all, we're young, we're legal (well, almost) and we're old enough to get into trouble! Who could resist?

We've been publishing outstanding novels for the past twenty years, and there are many more where those came from. Don't miss upcoming books by your favorite authors: Vicki Lewis Thompson, Kate Hoffmann, Kristine Rolofson, Jill Shalvis and Leslie Kelly. And Harlequin Temptation has always offered talented new authors to add to your collection. In the next few months look for stories from some of these exciting new finds: Emily McKay, Tanya Michaels, Cami Dalton and Mara Fox.

To celebrate our birthday, we're bringing back one of our most popular miniseries, Editor's Choice. Whenever we have a book that's new, innovative, *extraordinary*, look for the Editor's Choice flash. And the first one's out this month! In *Cover Me*, talented Stephanie Bond tells the hilarious tale of a native New Yorker who finds herself out of her element and loving it. Written totally in the first person, *Cover Me* is a real treat. And don't miss the rest of this month's irresistible offerings—a naughty Wrong Bed book by Jill Shalvis, another installment of the True Blue Calhouns by Julie Kistler and a delightful Valentine tale by Kate Hoffmann.

So, come be a part of the next generation of Harlequin Temptation. We might be a little wild, but we're having a whole lot of fun. And who knows—some of the thrill might rub off....

Enjoy,

Brenda Chin
Associate Senior Editor
Harlequin Temptation

JILL SHALVIS

BACK IN THE BEDROOM

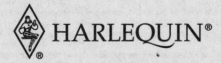

HARLEQUIN®

TORONTO • NEW YORK • LONDON
AMSTERDAM • PARIS • SYDNEY • HAMBURG
STOCKHOLM • ATHENS • TOKYO • MILAN • MADRID
PRAGUE • WARSAW • BUDAPEST • AUCKLAND

ISBN 0-373-69162-9

BACK IN THE BEDROOM

Copyright © 2004 by Jill Shalvis.

This edition published by arrangement with Harlequin Books S.A.

® and TM are trademarks of the publisher. Trademarks indicated with
® are registered in the United States Patent and Trademark Office, the
Canadian Trade Marks Office and in other countries.

Visit us at www.eHarlequin.com

Printed in U.S.A.

A NOTE FROM THE AUTHOR...

I love books where the hero and heroine are forced into proximity right from the get-go. So I really had fun with this heroine who walks into a burglary and ends up locked in a tiny room with a tall, gorgeous man without his clothes. Tessa and Reilly have one thing in common—they want out. Only, a little thing happens along the way...this almost unbearable attraction.

I feel really fortunate to be included in the twentieth anniversary along with some good friends. Happy birthday, Temptation!

Happy reading,

Jill Shalvis

P.S. I love to hear from readers! Visit my Web site at www.jillshalvis.com.

Books by Jill Shalvis

1

TESSA DELACANTRO ALWAYS PAID her taxes, ate at least one serving of fruit or veggies a day and generally was a rule follower. But that didn't mean she didn't yearn for adventure.

In fact, she yearned a lot.

It was why she'd agreed to watch her boss's posh house in La Canada for the weekend while he took his latest fling to Cabo San Lucas.

Tessa had her own place but it didn't have ten thousand square feet or cable or even a degree of poshness, so she looked forward to living like the rich and famous for two nights. As an Art History major without a lot of prospects in the field, she'd spent the past few years as an office clerk here and there, doing some accounting, doing some secretarial work, learning how to run Microsoft programs without crashing anyone's system.

What she hadn't done was figure out how to work in any of that adventure and excitement she wanted, but this was California, *Southern* California, to boot. The land of opportunity. She was open to anything, and liked to keep her options free. She had high hopes for her latest job as a temp in an agency run by the colorful Eddie Ledger. The sharp, debonair, electrifying man had a myriad of businesses in his empire, most of which ran themselves, leaving him free to do things like go to Cabo on a whim.

She could get into that lifestyle. She parked her car at the top of Eddie's long, curvy driveway, which protected the Tudor-style mansion from view of the street. It had a beautiful yellow-and-white front, with flowers everywhere, lining the grass and steps to the porch.

Letting herself in with the key Eddie had given her, she dropped her purse and keys on the tiled foyer that was bigger than her entire apartment and sighed. From here she could see the large living room and so many windows showing off stunning views of the Angeles Crest Mountains she felt a little dizzy.

Or maybe it was a lack of food. She'd come right from a long day of work and hadn't yet grabbed dinner, so she headed in, looking for the kitchen. Eddie wouldn't mind—her tall, dark and outrageously handsome boss had told her to help herself. He might be as sly as a fox and extremely fond of women, but when it came to his employees, he was sweet and warm and extremely kind.

The kitchen took her breath away. She took in the custom-made maple cabinetry, the granite counters and the Sub-Zero maple-faced fridge. The secret chef inside her salivated.

Her own kitchen could have fit inside the brand-spanking-new Russell six-burner range. If she wasn't so tired, she'd run back out to the grocery store and get a bunch of exciting ingredients, then come back and cook away. It'd be fun if she had a date to cook for, but she didn't. Maybe she'd call her sister to come over and they'd watch the new 007 movie. They could sigh and eat, eat and sigh....

Her footsteps echoed as she crossed the granite tiles, warm from the setting sun beaming in through the myriad of windows here, too. She reached for the handle on the fridge, just to get a quick snack, but hesitated at the loud thump that definitely wasn't her stomach growling. With a frown, she headed out of the kitchen, back into the huge, open living room, and looked down the wide, oak-lined hallway that arched off to the left and vanished.

Someone was down there.

The maid, maybe, but Tessa wasn't sure Eddie had a maid. In any case, she wasn't going to take any chances. La Canada residents were snooty and into their privacy. This house was no exception. Heavily wooded and a bit secluded, she could scream until the cows came home and no one would hear. At home in Glendale—only a few minutes from here, but a world away as far as neighborhoods went—she'd have grabbed her trusty baseball bat and the phone to call the police.

No baseball bat here, and at first glance around the fancy place, she couldn't even find a telephone. But she'd seen plenty of horror flicks in her twenty-six years, and had no intention of being the stupid chick. She'd just get out of the house and *then* call the police.

The front door seemed extremely far away so she whirled to the sliding glass door behind her instead. But she stopped short when she remembered she'd left her keys on the foyer floor with her purse. She needed those keys for an escape.

And then came another thump.

Spooked, she started running toward the foyer. Track had been her least-favorite sport, but she managed to move like lightning. Funny what fear did for motivation. Ten-thousand square feet was suddenly *far* too much space, and she felt grateful for her perpetual poverty and six-hundred square feet of closed-in apartment that would have only taken a blink of an eye to run through—

"Excuse me."

The male voice sounded so polite, coming from behind her, that she actually stopped short and looked over her shoulder.

And faced a man carrying a DVD player. He looked to be twenty-something, and wore jeans and a grungy white thermal shirt on his large, beefy body. With a grimace, he set down the DVD player and straightened. "Another visitor. Terrific." He cracked his knuckles and suddenly looked exceptionally big and menacing. He gestured with a jerk of his chin toward the back of the house. "Okay, sweetcakes, let's go."

She took a step back and shook her head.

He sent a frustrated glance heavenward. "Why me? Look, just tell me you're not a martial arts expert like the other guy."

She eyed the growing bruise on his cheekbone and took another careful step backward. Gee, only fifty more and she'd make it. "What are you doing here while Eddie's out of town?"

"I'm here to mess the place up." His voice was pure annoyance. A put-out bear of a man. "And I get to take whatever I want while I'm at it. Those are my orders. If he's out of town, so much the better."

"G-go ahead, I'll...just wait outside." She took another step, wondering if he could see that she was shaking like a leaf. Forty-nine more steps...

He shook his big head. "Don't even bother. We both know I'm not going to let you go until I'm done here and long gone, so I'll repeat myself. *This way*."

Step forty-eight—

"Goddammit." He lumbered after her.

Whirling, she ordered her feet to move. Forty-seven, forty-six— An arm hooked around her neck, hauling her back against a rock-hard body, withholding her inherent right to breathe. She opened her mouth to scream, but he slapped a hand against her mouth and nose—she definitely wasn't breathing any time soon. Lifting her off her feet, he started walking.

Spots danced in front of her eyes. Out of pure des-

peration for air, she reached back and grabbed a hand-
ful of his hair.

"Ouch! Holy shit, lady!" He gripped her wrist and
jerked it down, squeezing her neck at the same time.

Her head was going to pop right off. The spots blossomed into full Technicolor, and now she had an aching wrist to go with them as he dragged her along, back
through the kitchen. Her life passed in front of her eyes;
her mom and dad, her sister and brother, her cute little
apartment where she cooked, read, lived…and then
without warning he let go of her and shoved.

She landed on a hard tile floor and spent a moment
on her hands and knees concentrating on dragging air
into her lungs. A door slammed and she jerked her
head up. It was nearly dark outside now and there
wasn't a light on in the small room she found herself in,
which was maybe eight feet by eight feet. But there did
appear to be a floodlight right outside the very small
window on the far wall. Thank goodness for timers,
she thought, and tried not to panic. Unlike the rest of
the house, this room was gray and bare. The only piece
of furniture in the place was a narrow cot—

Oh God. A narrow cot that was filled with the prone
body of a man wearing nothing but black knit boxers.
Long, sleek and powerful, there wasn't an inch of excess on him. Even in the meager light she could see he
was sinewy, lean and hard, and she took him all in, including the myriad of interesting scars like the long,
jagged one on his right pec, and another small puck-

ered one—like a bullet wound?—low on his flat, corrugated belly.

Still breathing like a misused racehorse, still shaky, she stared at him as he groaned, slowly sat up and blinked.

So did she, because he was the spitting image of her boss—the forty-nine-year-old, gorgeous Eddie Ledger—only younger and far more serious than she'd ever seen the perpetually smiling Eddie—

He staggered to his feet and put a hand to the back of his head, then pulled it away and stared at his fingers, which came away sticky with...she blinked in the dim light. Blood. Oh God. She really didn't do well with blood—

"Who are you?" he demanded.

Given the force of his voice, he wasn't mortally injured. And given the incredible sharpness of his eyes and body, he wasn't the type to be easily laid flat. She stood there uneasily, not sure who were the good guys and who were the bad. But this man, this six-foot-tall, lean, mean, nearly naked fighting machine looked so much like her boss....

His laser, light-blue eyes looked her over, then met her gaze, and she swallowed hard. Had she really thought he looked like Eddie? Maybe the dark, spiky hair, the see-through eyes, the lean, shadowed jaw were the same, but even though she'd never seen Eddie nearly naked, she doubted he had such a hard, muscled, sleek look to him. He'd certainly never looked so intense, so unsmiling, so utterly edgy and terrifying in the month she'd been working for him.

Suddenly her last job, doing payroll for a local YMCA, didn't seem so bad. If only they hadn't had to reduce their staff, if only she hadn't been the low person on the totem pole, if only...

"Who are you?" he repeated in that low, husky voice that would have resembled Eddie's, if it didn't have all the fury in it.

"T-Tessa Delacantro." For the second time in a few minutes, she backed to a door. The handle hit her fingers and she jerked at it, but it didn't budge.

"It's locked, and like everything else in the house, it's the best money can buy so it can't be broken," Eddie's evil twin said.

She tried it again anyway, still eyeing him carefully. How many times had her sister told her ninety-nine percent of all men were scum? Not that she'd ever listened.

If she ever got out of here, she'd listen to Carolyn. *Always.*

He had one hand propped up against the wall as he contemplated her with an enigmatic expression that was probably supposed to be polite, not terrifying.

But he didn't have the facial features for polite, not with those shocking light eyes and harsh frown. "What are you doing here?"

She tried not to stare, but it wasn't every day she was so up close and personal to a nearly naked man while shaking in fear. In fact, she was hardly *ever* this close to a nearly naked man, scared or otherwise. "I'm watching the house for the weekend," she said. "But... Eddie?"

A short, rough laugh escaped him at that, a sound that had nothing to do with mirth. "No."

Her heart was flinging itself against her ribs so hard it was amazing they hadn't all cracked. "Um..." She swallowed hard. "Eddie's brother? Eddie's...twin brother?"

His go-to-hell eyes frosted over. "No. I'm Reilly." Body taut with tension, arms crossed now—which delineated his hard contours in interesting ways, not that she was noticing—he let out a breath. "His son."

Eddie had told her he had a son, but by the indulgent smile on his face when he'd mentioned him, Tessa had imagined a little boy, certainly someone far younger than thirtyish and not quite so mind-bogglingly magnificent. "But—" She let out a sound of pure confusion and eyed the window. The place had been built on a hill, and naturally, she was hillside and at least forty feet up.

She looked at Reilly again. His stance implied strength and an innate confidence she could only dream of. There was no doubt, this man was in complete control of himself, even injured and half-naked.

Apparently unconcerned with that nakedness, he moved toward her. She flinched back against the door, but he kept coming, and took the hand she'd unconsciously held to her still-raw and aching throat.

Slowly but inexorably he pulled her hand up and stared at what he'd exposed.

Impossibly, his eyes hardened even more. "They hurt you, too." He ran a finger over her skin then lifted his gaze to hers. "You were to watch the house for Eddie?"

"Yes."

He made a rough sound. "That figures."

"Figures how?"

"He favors the young and innocent."

The words "young and innocent" came out as if those were the most irritating traits a person could have. How many times had she been told she looked ten years younger than her twenty-six? Plenty. So she looked young, big deal. Did people always have to use the word *innocent* when describing her?

She really resented the hell out of that.

"You interrupted them," he guessed, and grimaced with what actually might have been concern. Then he took her other hand as well, the one she'd been cradling to her belly because her wrist still hurt, and turned it over to expose the mottled bruising already appearing there. He lifted his gaze and held hers for a long moment. "Where else did they get you?"

"Nowhere."

Still holding her wrist, he looked her over thoroughly, and she let him because she didn't feel up to doing anything else.

Besides, he had the air of a man well used to being in charge, the kind of man others would look to in a crisis. The kind of man that would be annoying in everyday life because of it.

Alpha male at its finest. And she preferred beta men. This guy didn't appear to have a sensitive, compassionate bone in his body. He certainly didn't feel the need to charm and cajole, or make everyone smile around him as his father did. He simply didn't have the same easy warmth and charisma.

And in truth, he actually seemed far more dangerous than the thug who'd thrown her in here. She wondered how anyone had ever managed to hurt him, because all that carefully restrained strength was intimidating as hell. He must have been ambushed, and she doubted he'd gone down easily.

And yet the way he was looking her over for unseen injuries softened something inside her, just a little, at least until he touched the back of his head again and cursed, which made her jump. "You're bleeding," she said inanely.

"Yeah, that's what happens when you take a heavy, ridiculously overpriced vase to the head."

He *had* been ambushed. "Sit down. Please—"

"I'm fine."

Well, he was indeed pretty darn fine, but wasn't it just like a man not to admit when he was hurt. She turned back to the door and wriggled the handle again. It still didn't give. At least her legs had stopped shaking. "Maybe we can somehow stop him, before he cleans Eddie out—"

"Are you kidding? No one can clean Eddie out, he's got more money than God."

"Well, we can't just stand here." She leaned against the door in frustration. This place was her responsibility this weekend and she took that responsibility seriously. "That guy said his job was to mess this place up. Maybe we can bang on the door, make nuisances of ourselves, until he comes back down here. Then one of us can distract him while the other—"

"You're as crazy as Eddie." He rubbed the back of his neck and let out a mirthless laugh. "And here's a news flash. There's *four* of them, all apparently intent on getting good old Dad's toys, of which he has many."

"*Four?*"

"I took two of them out and was working on the third when the last one knocked me on the head from behind." He gritted his teeth, his jaw tight. "I'd have gotten him, too, but they caught me distracted."

Tessa's mouth had fallen open. There'd been four of them. And he'd taken out three.

By himself.

She eyed his bare chest only inches from her nose and tried not to ogle. "So you're the martial arts expert the guy was grumbling about."

He nodded.

"What happened to your clothes?"

He looked away. "When I hit the floor, they found my gun."

"Your...gun."

"And then they strip-searched me for more weapons."

She could only stare at him. She'd imagined him dangerous. Edgy. But...armed? "Wow."

He ground his teeth but didn't say anything else.

"Four," she repeated softly.

"And now two of them are armed," he said. "Courtesy of *moi*. So even if we could distract them and bring them back this way, it's not the wisest move. Unless you're wearing a bulletproof vest...? No?" he asked when she shook her head. "See, bad move." Gingerly, as if he had a headache, which he no doubt did, he sank back to the cot.

"Who would do this?"

He lifted a shoulder. "Your guess is as good as mine. Eddie certainly has plenty of enemies."

How was that possible? The Eddie she knew wouldn't harm a fly. "So we're just going to stand here and wait for them to decide we're not exactly an asset?"

"I'm not going to stand." He lay back, put his feet up, and closed his eyes.

She stared at him. "You're not serious."

He drew in a deep breath, and, as if they were attached to his body by strings, her eyes followed the motion of his broad chest rising and falling, followed the way his six-pack belly caved in, and how his knit boxers lovingly cupped his...package.

And, oh my, what a package.

A little shocked at herself, she turned her back on him. "I can't believe this." She took a good look around the small, spartan room. There was nothing in it but the cot, and yet the rest of the house was so absolutely beautifully done. It was strange. "Where are we anyway?"

"The servants' quarters."

She turned around to look at him, but he hadn't budged nor opened his eyes. "Did you grow up here?"

"No."

"Did you—"

"How many more questions do you figure you have, because I'd like to sleep off this headache."

She'd been manhandled, terrified and trapped, and she could deal with that. But it would have been nice if it'd happened with a warmer, more compassionate man, a man who put others' needs and fears ahead of his own need for a nap.

Certainly someone more in touch with his own emotions.

In other words, this man's polar opposite. "You shouldn't go to sleep," she said, unable to just ignore him. She had a feeling he could be fully dressed and she still wouldn't be able to ignore him. "You could be concussed."

He didn't answer. His body took up the entire cot

and more, a good portion of his long legs were hanging off the cot. His wide shoulders barely fit onto the thin mattress.

But what if *she'd* wanted to lie down? What then? She'd have to be snuggled right up against all that bare sinewy flesh.

Not that he'd even care, as he appeared to not have given her a second thought. Wasn't that ever so flattering? "Are you really going to sleep?"

"Shhh."

Unbelievable. She watched him breathe slowly and evenly for another moment before letting out a frustrated sigh. "Fine. Sleep." Without a care to her own possible fears and pain. Wasn't that just like an alpha?

She eyed the room again. The window was still too small, with no fire escape or way to climb down. Interestingly enough though, there appeared to be an attic access in the ceiling, a decent-sized one, too. Not that she could reach it alone, but they had to get out. Maybe if he helped— "Reilly?"

He let out a long-suffering sigh. "What?"

"I have another option than sleep."

He opened his eyes, the look in them blatantly sexual. "Oh, yeah?"

Oh boy, definitely alpha. Extremely alpha. So why his low, husky tone and those suggestive words made her body tingle, she hadn't a clue.

"What did you have in mind?" His voice dripped an earthy sensuality.

"Uh..." Oddly enough, the only thing she had in mind right now was X-rated. "I forgot."

His gaze ran over her from head to toe, flared with heat, shocking her, before he closed his eyes. "Okay, then."

Okay, then.

2

REILLY DRIFTED off pleasantly, to a place where his head didn't hurt and he was wearing clothes—

"*Reilly.*" This extremely loud whisper was accompanied by a shove at his shoulder.

She was ba-a-ack. His father's latest fling, the petite pixie with the shoulder-length brown hair and mossy-green eyes that flashed her every thought for the world to see.

Was she even of legal age?

"Reilly?"

He had no idea why she bothered to whisper, when she was doing it so loudly she could have woken the dead.

"I think you should wake up now," she said, and added another teeth-rattling shake. "Come on. Get up and count to ten or something."

Honest to God, the woman talked more than any woman he'd ever met.

"Just to make sure you don't go into a coma." Another shake. "It's only been five minutes but I can't remember how long you're supposed to let someone with a bleeding head injury sleep."

"I'm not in a coma," he said with his eyes still closed. It wasn't really sleep he was interested in, but a way to pass the time other than looking at the oddly sweet and sexy Tessa. "And my head is no longer bleeding."

"I still don't think you should sleep."

All those years in the army and then the CIA, one thing had stuck with him—how to catch quality Zs in five short little minutes. He'd rather have had longer than five minutes. Say the whole night, so the time would have passed painlessly, but slowly he opened his eyes, staring into her wide green ones. "I'm fine."

"How many fingers am I holding up?" She wriggled three in front of his nose.

He grabbed them. "I'm fine," he repeated.

"Fine enough to go up the attic access in the ceiling? I think it has good escape potential."

In the meager but adequate light he took in her slight little form bending over him, her hand on his chest. Not that he minded a woman's fingers on him, but his head felt like it was going to roll right off his shoulders. And if she shoved him one more time, yet again jarring his head, he was going to roll her pretty little body beneath his to hold her still. "Escape potential," he repeated, and she smiled at him and nodded.

"All you have to do is climb up. Then shimmy your way through whatever is up there, and drop down through another access in another room. *Voilà*, escape. I know you said you didn't grow up here, but you could probably find a phone, right?"

He'd had his cell on him, before he'd made the mistake of actually coming here to see Eddie. Before he'd knocked out three of the four idiots, then realized too late there was one more idiot behind him. Suddenly, he'd seen stars from the hit with a vase probably worth enough to feed a small country.

Which made *him* the idiot.

And to think, all he'd wanted was to tell his father to knock it off, to stop sending sexy little temps to his office and to stop sending him messages to come visit.

Instead, he'd ended up on the wrong end of a strip search, being held hostage by his own gun no less. He, a guy who knew how to kill a man in more ways than he could count, had been taken down by a few punks with a vendetta against his father.

If that didn't bite, watching them mess with his gun while he sat in his shorts sure did. And if that didn't also say how much he'd lost his edge, how dead-on-target his decision had been to get out of the CIA, he didn't know what did.

He supposed it could have been worse.

They could have killed him.

"Can you? Find a phone?"

The cute young thing was still talking. He let out a long breath and opened his eyes. "Probably."

"So...will you?"

"No."

She blinked. "What?"

"No," he repeated clearly.

"But...why not?"

"Because it's dark."

She eyed him from head to toe, making him glad he'd been allowed to keep his shorts because for some reason, even though she drove him crazy, his body didn't seem to want to agree with his brain on that assessment.

"The dark shouldn't bother a guy like you," she finally said.

Think again, sweetheart. "I'll go at daylight."

"But..."

"Daylight. Now...was there something you wanted to do to pass the time?"

"No," she squeaked.

"Fine." He tried to forget he was stuck with one of his father's babes. She looked like heaven, he'd give her that, but she talked too much. At the ripe old age of thirty-one, Reilly had come to realize he liked women, he liked them a lot, but he liked them quiet, reserved and controlled...much like himself, actually.

But this one couldn't be quiet to save her life, much less be restrained and controlled. She was pacing the floor right this very second. "We're not going to get out of here for a few hours, so you might as well stop wearing a hole in that tile."

She stopped and looked at him as if he'd lost his mind.

And in truth, maybe he had. Certainly the old Reilly

would have gotten up and rescued the damsel in distress.

The new Reilly, no longer of CIA, no longer of anything or anyone else except Reilly Ledger of Accountant-4-Hire, his small accounting firm with clients as reclusive as he was. He pushed papers around when and how he felt like it, didn't take orders from anyone but himself, and never, ever rescued damsels in distress.

Unless it was accounting-related, and, in that case, he charged by the hour.

She put her hands on her hips, a gesture it appeared she used a lot to compensate for being so short, but it did draw his attention to her mid-thigh sundress. It was pale-green with flowers on it and was actually quite demure, except that every time she moved it danced around her tanned, toned legs.

Very distracting, those legs.

"There's no good reason why we have to stay in here," she said.

"Other than we're trapped?"

"Honestly, all you have to do is crawl through—"

"I said no."

She crossed her arms, plumping up the breasts he imagined could use a little plumping. "Give me one good reason other than you won't be able to see."

He stretched, and winced at the ache at the base of his skull. "That's the reason."

She stared at him, then tilted her head up and eyed the access, which was indeed wide enough for his body, and indeed a most excellent escape route. "You can't be afraid of the dark." She shook her head. "No. I don't buy it. That would make you a sensitive man, and frankly, I'm not getting a lot of sensitivity here."

"You're not getting out tonight."

"Fine, if you don't want to do it. I will." She dropped her arms and straightened, visibly swallowing while she mustered up all her courage. If he hadn't been pissed and hurting, he might have admired her.

"Boost me up," she said.

From flat on his back, he laughed, his first all night. "Let me get this straight. You'll go crawling through the attic in the pitch dark, drop into a room you don't know, possibly into the waiting arms of the guy I didn't knock out, and then what? Let them have another stab at you?"

Her determined expression faltered, and the terror came through. "You're right," she whispered. "This is really serious, and I think it's just hitting me. I'm sorry." Then she blinked those wide, expressive eyes and hugged herself. He felt like a jerk.

He closed his eyes. "You're just going to have to wait. Eddie will figure out you're missing and come looking for you."

"He's in Cabo with his girlfriend for two days."

That had his eyes opening again. "I thought *you,* Statutory Rape Lawsuit Walking, were the girlfriend."

"You— I—" She sputtered, then laughed. She laughed hard and so genuinely, he actually felt the knot loosen in his belly because she was being honest, which meant his father hadn't seduced this woman who was too cute and too young for him.

"I'm twenty-six years old," she finally informed him. "Quite legal. And not that this is any of your business, but I am *not* your father's girlfriend. I work in his temp agency."

"Ah." He didn't want to think about why that made him feel a lot better, so he closed his eyes again.

A thunk sounded and with a sigh, he cracked open an eye. Looking small and defenseless, she'd sat on the floor against the far wall, beside the locked door, still hugging herself. Her knees were up, her head down on her arms.

Fine. That was a good place for her, far away from him, with her mouth thankfully shut for once.

He might have been able to pretend he was somewhere else other than lying on a damn cot with no clothes and a bump on the back of his head...if she hadn't shivered.

He closed his eyes against it but he could have sworn he could hear her teeth rattling together. "Damn it. Get over here."

She lifted her head, and in the glow from the light outside the window, he saw her expression. Gone was the temporary bravado. Gone were all signs that she was holding up under what even he could admit had been a fairly traumatizing experience. Wet now, her eyes were the color of rain-soaked leaves, and her mouth trembled. The bruises on her throat had blossomed.

Hell. "You all right?"

"Give me a minute." She scrubbed her hands over her face. "I know I'm talking, talking, talking, but that's nerves and fear. I'll try to stop, I promise."

Slowly he sat up. No dizziness, which he figured was a good thing, so he risked standing. Barefoot, bare everything except the essentials, he took the few steps that brought him close. "You take the cot."

She stared at his knees and shook her head.

"Tessa."

She ignored him. Since he'd been trying to ignore her for half an hour now, he understood and appreciated the sentiment. But it was possible she was going into delayed shock, and that even he couldn't ignore, as his training was too ingrained. He hunkered down beside her and, wanting to check her pulse, reached for her wrist.

Startled, she jerked back and into the wall, crying out at the contact and wincing away from him at the same time.

"Go away," she whispered, mortified to find her eyes spilling over. But he'd scared her, and she really hated that. Before tonight, nothing had scared her.

"Hey." Lifting his hands, watching her from those light, light eyes, he spoke softly. "It's just me."

"I know." And she did, but it was just that for one bad moment, she'd been transported back into Eddie's

living room, back to that guy in the dirty long underwear shirt, and he'd been reaching for her—

Reilly took her hand. "Just me," he repeated very
quietly.

"I know that."

"I want you to lie down and try to relax."

"Relax." She bit back her hysterical laughter. "Sure.
I'll relax."

"Great, because you're wound up tighter than a
clock."

"Yes, well, this hasn't been exactly a good day."

"I know." He contemplated her in silence for a
while. "Are you cold?"

Yes. She was cold. And hungry. And tired. And, apparently, letting this whole situation really get to her.

"Come on," he said. Still on his knees before her, he
wriggled his fingers, clearly indicating she could take
his hand.

Tessa closed her eyes. She didn't want to take his
hand. She wanted to crawl in a hole and have a meltdown. She wanted to be alone while doing it, thank
you very much. "Go to sleep," she said.

"I can't do that now," said the contrary man.

Of course not. Because heaven forbid one thing go
her way tonight.

3

"TESSA, COME ON. Lie down."

Only a moment ago she'd been holding it together just fine, and then Reilly had to come close with that long, sleekly muscled body glowing in the faint light and go all sweet and sensitive on her.

Ha! As if he could ever even pretend to be sweet and sensitive.

"Come on," he said gently. *Gently.*

Didn't he know that was how to break a woman down—show a tender insight and perception, along with near nudity so magnificent it made her mouth water?

"Tessa?"

And the way he said her name in that low, husky voice... It brought to mind hot summer nights and satin sheets and wild but sweet lovemaking.

Not that she knew much about hot summer nights combined with satin sheets and wild but sweet lovemaking, but a girl had her fantasies.

And he was a walking fantasy.

Taking her hand in his, he rose. "Up you go." He led her to the cot with a hand at the small of her back. As if he was kind and compassionate. "Lie down right here."

No questions at the end of his sentences, not for Reilly. Nope, he never said, "Okay?" or "Would you like?" He was a guy, through and through, and an extremely confident one at that. Not to mention demanding, because really, why ask when clearly he knew everything?

"Tess. Lie down."

He shortened her name. No one else had ever done that, and it seemed...extremely intimate, and on his lips, almost unbearably sexy.

Suddenly the room felt so small, too small. She needed wide open space and she needed it now. Forget adventure, had she ever said she wanted adventure like this? No! She wanted her cozy little apartment, her sister's nightly visit bearing ice cream and a good movie. Maybe a call from her brother just to say hi.

"Sit."

She shivered again—what was the matter with her? She was safe, she was fine, and *now* she was going to fall apart? But she sat on the cot. It wasn't as soft as it looked, and didn't have any covers on it. "I don't understand this room," she said, and shivered again, knowing she was talking out of nervous reaction, but unable to help herself. "The rest of the house is so beautiful and warm and comfortable."

Reilly looked around him and shrugged. "For all Eddie's wild and extravagant living, he doesn't like servants—it's the subservient thing, I guess. At least ones who don't sleep in his bedroom. Fixing this room would be a waste of his time, he probably never even uses it."

He talked about Eddie as though he didn't like him. She didn't understand that either. "Your father is a wonderful man."

"What does that have to do with the fact he goes through women like some of us go through water?"

Since she couldn't deny that, she lay down and curled on her side facing away from him. "I'm not a bed hog. You can have half."

"It's not big enough."

Fine. No skin off her nose. Tessa planned to lie there and wait for dawn, but the late hour, combined with her heavy workweek, not to mention the evening's events, had taken a greater toll than she'd imagined, and miraculously, she drifted off...

Only to dream about being grabbed from behind, about the thick, muscled forearm cutting off her air—

She jerked straight off the cot and gasped for the breath to scream but when she blinked into focus the small, rather dark room and the silent man standing there propping up the far wall, she sagged.

"Just a dream," he said.

Imagine that.

"Go back to sleep."

Right. She sat down, and realized she was chilled to the bone.

"Sleep," he said. "Not sit."

"I'm cold."

He tipped his head back and glanced at the ceiling as if seeking divine intervention. He moved forward until his knees bumped the cot. "There's no blanket."

"No." She wrapped her arms around herself and kept her eyes straight ahead, which landed them...oh, only about eye level with the best-looking male stomach ever.

"Lie down."

She had no idea why she obeyed him, but with another shiver, she did, and then went flat onto her back, where she held her breath as he lowered himself onto the cot as well. He lay on his side facing her. He held up his head with his hand, setting his other very lightly on her stomach.

Her belly quivered. Other parts did, too, and she looked for a diversion. She found it in the closed access above them. If only he'd just climb up there—

His fingers tightened on her and he leaned in, just a little. "*Sleep.*"

Right. Since his broad shoulders, chest and amazing eyes filled her vision, she closed her eyes. Only problem, without a visual, her other senses kicked in. His scent came to her, a little soapy, a little woodsy and a lot male. His heat and strength seemed to seep into her chilled bones and, helplessly, she relaxed a bit, because maybe, just maybe, he really was kind and sweet and sensitive behind all that...

"You don't snore do you?"

Her eyes flew open. "No. Do you?"

"No." He lowered his head to the cot and closed his eyes.

Hmm. New problem. Now their faces were only an inch apart. He hadn't shaved in a few days, she guessed, given the shadow on his lean jaw. He had the longest, darkest eyelashes. A complete waste on a man, especially this man. There was a white jagged scar running along one eyebrow, another high on his forehead. Where had he gotten such scars? His nose was long and straight, his mouth fixed in a grim, hard line. His dark hair was so short it stood straight up, and she imagined he rarely bothered with a comb. She wondered if it was soft or—

"Are you going to think this loudly all night?" he asked, but then another shiver wracked her and he let out a long breath. "Okay, but only in the name of shared body heat..." He gripped her around the waist and tugged, turning her at the same time, until she was snuggled firmly against him, her spine to his chest, the backs of her legs to the front of his and all the spots in between perfectly aligned. All in the "name of shared body heat."

Oh boy.

She tried to go to sleep, she really did. It proved an impossibility while she was holding her breath as she was. Behind her, Reilly lay utterly silent, utterly still, not pressing any of his...parts...against her unduly.

And she'd already noticed he had parts. Oh my, did he have parts.

Scooting free so that she could roll onto her back and look at him, she instantly wished she hadn't. He was so close, and so warm and well...sexy as hell.

And also annoyed, very annoyed.

"I'm sorry," she whispered. "It's just that...it's all hitting me." She was horrified to hear her voice waver and blamed it on adrenaline. Anyone would be feeling it, she assured herself. "It's making my mind rush and my body shake, and I hate that. I don't mean to keep you up, but I can't stop wondering."

"Wondering what?"

"Are they still out there, and what if they decide to come back—"

He put a finger to her lips and waited. When she didn't try to talk around him, his mouth curved. "There. See if you can hold still, just like that."

She grabbed his wrist and freed her mouth. "I realize that you can turn off the feelings and emotions with ease, but I can't. I'm scared, if you want the truth, and I'm feeling a little claustrophobic here. I want..."

His eyes heated. "What?"

"Comfort," she whispered, and trembled again, her body betraying her, which really made her mad.

A sigh rumbled from him and he settled one big hand at her hip and pulled her closer. *There.* The comfort she'd wanted. Yet with him looking down at her with that disconcerting gaze, with his body so close, so big and warm and unintentionally sexy—and it was unintentional, she knew he wasn't trying to drive her crazy—what she felt was far, far from comfort. In an almost out-of-body experience, she whispered his name in a voice no longer quivering with trepidation but with something else entirely.

Something that felt shockingly like...hunger. Need.

She had no idea what was happening to her but it was so much better than being afraid. Infinitely better than the cold. She came up onto her side, so that they were once again body-to-body, only now face-to-face. Reaching up, she slowly slid her hand around the back of his neck and tugged him closer.

His fingers, in the act of gently skimming up and down her hip in the name of shared body heat and comfort, froze. "Tess—"

If this was a dream, she didn't want to wake up. If it was indeed an out-of-body experience, she wouldn't complain, but something made her put her mouth to the very corner of his.

He held perfectly still. Unnaturally still but she didn't care. The connection of their mouths had spread warmth through her like nothing else ever had, so she nibbled at the other side, too. Adrenaline? Fear? She didn't know, didn't care, because the ball of warmth deep inside her started smoking now. To stoke it into a full-blown fire, she opened her mouth and took his bottom lip in her teeth.

This wrenched a deep rumble from his throat, a

warning from the beast, which should have stopped her, would have in any other place and time, but not tonight.

"Tessa. This is—"

Crazy. She knew that. Just as she knew it was the events of the night making her feel this way, but she didn't care. She settled her mouth on his, hoping he'd give into it, too, so that she wasn't the only fool.

But Reilly was still rigid, holding himself back with a restraint that she'd admire another time. For now she arched against him, enough to know that his thin shorts couldn't hide what he was beginning to feel.

"Tess—" he growled with unmistakable warning.

Nope, she didn't want him to talk. Not now. She opened her lips and touched her tongue to the corner of his mouth, and in doing so, finally, *finally* unleashed the beast.

He dove headfirst into the kiss then, wrapping his arms around her body and bringing it more snugly to his, thrusting a muscled thigh between hers, opening his mouth wide for a hot, deep, wet kiss that would surely highlight her dreams instead of the nightmares this day had afforded her.

Oh, yes, this was perfect. This was just what the doctor had ordered for her shock. She slid her fingers into his hair, taking notice that it *was* soft, as not very much else of him was. Her other hand went on a tour of his tight shoulders and solid chest, feeling the smooth glide of muscle beneath skin, and she knew if she had all night it wouldn't be long enough.

Given how he held her, with the fingers of one hand spread wide, holding her head for the sexy forays of his plundering tongue, Reilly felt the same. His other hand skimmed over her hip, her belly and ribs, so that his long fingers rested just beneath her breast.

More, she thought. She had to have more, she had to feel his touch. Straining against him, she slid down an inch, just enough to have those fingers of his brushing the very underside of her breast, and she let out a sigh of pleasure.

At the sound, he moved of his own accord, cupping her breast in his big hand, rasping his thumb over her nipple and making her toes curl.

She wanted out of her clothes and she wanted him out of his. She wanted to be skin-to-skin, wanted to feel all his impressive strength and heat against her so that she could forget what had happened to her earlier, what could still happen.

Just thinking it made her let out a little cry, and he pulled her closer. "Shh," he murmured. "Just me. Just you and me..." He danced a hand up her spine, then down again, until she relaxed into him once more, until she was clinging and back on her way to the mindlessness she needed desperately. Then he had her bottom cupped in his palm, pressing her against an impressive erection she wanted cradled more firmly between her aching thighs. Oh, yes.

To get more, she hooked a leg over his, opening herself up so that he could thrust against her, and he did, one glorious thrust, before he went utterly, totally, carefully still.

Lifting his head, he stared down at her mouth, his breathing not nearly as steady as it had been.

"That was quite a bedtime story," he said, and flipped her over again, to her other side, so that she could no longer see his face.

"But..."

"Shh," he said again.

She ground her teeth. "I can't *shh*."

"Yes, you can."

"But...don't you want more?"

His laugh was low and mirthless. "Hell, yes."

"Well, then—"

"It's not going to happen, Tess."

"Reilly—"

He reached an arm over her shoulder and put his fingers against her mouth. "Shh."

How could he just turn it off? She squirmed a little, and felt his erection against her bottom.

So he hadn't just turned it off at all. "But—"

"Be good and go to sleep."

Be good?

Go to sleep?

Was he kidding? The man kissed like no one she'd ever met, touched like no one she'd ever met, and he thought she could just turn it off and go to sleep? "Reilly..."

A soft snore sounded in her ear, making her want to scream in frustration. She couldn't decide if she hated him or wanted him. Her body was still humming and twitching, so that meant she wanted him, but he'd firmly set her away as if it'd been nothing.

Definitely she hated him, she decided.

Eventually she set her head down on his arm and tried to follow him into slumberland. As far as pillows went, he wasn't soft and giving, but he sure was warm and smelled like heaven.

And—this was such a terrible thought she couldn't even believe she'd had it—she was glad he'd been stripped, because feeling his body against hers could take her mind off her troubles as nothing else could.

Unless, of course, he'd kept kissing her.

4

REILLY AWOKE to a jostling that made his head hurt all over again. For a brief flash, he thought he was on a mission and it had all gone really, really bad.

A feeling he knew all too well.

He opened his eyes and promptly wished he hadn't.

It had most definitely gone really, really bad. It was still dark outside, but that hadn't stopped Tessa from standing on the cot at his feet and jumping up and down, trying to open the attic access herself, which stayed stubbornly out of her reach by a good six inches.

He did find himself sidetracked as the wide skirt on her sundress flew high on her thighs with each leap, but not even the quick flash of light-blue lace panties could help the hammering at the base of his skull.

Still, he watched for a long moment. Up and down. Up and down. And as she jumped, she turned so that she was no longer facing him, leaving him to notice that with each leap, those light-blue lace panties rose a little higher on those rounded cheeks of hers. She had quite a wedgie going.

"Not helping my head," he finally said, and startled, she whipped around to face him again, then lost her balance and fell to her knees onto the cot, using his chest as a grip.

Automatically he reached for her, steadied her and she sprawled out against him, slipping her arms around his body with an ease that bewildered him. She stared, apparently enraptured by whatever expression he wore on his face, making him wonder if he'd let his lusty thoughts show.

"Are we going to kiss again?" she whispered.

Oh, yes, he'd definitely let his thoughts show. Plus, now there was a hopeful quality to her voice that made him want to groan. Instead he ruthlessly tugged her skirt down as far as it would stretch over her thighs. No more visuals of that squeezable ass. "No."

"Because—"

"*No.*"

Kissing had been a really bad idea. Now that he'd tasted her, it was hard—no pun intended—to get the thought out of his brain, and other parts as well.

"I'm really going crazy," she whispered.

Yeah, well. Join the club.

"I need out." She made a fist against his chest and speared him with a frustrated glance. "How can you not need out?"

Simple. Just the thought of being enclosed in that dark attic, of how it would remind him of his last mission and how it had all gone bad, made him break out into a sweat.

"Reilly?" Her fingertips ran lightly over his shoulders.

He wasn't used to being touched, not like this. Give him a good fight, give him good sex, those were the kinds of touch he was used to.

"If we can't get out, if we have to stay here, then I have to talk," she said. "I have to hear *you* talk."

"I'm not much on talking."

She laughed, and the sound went through him like wine. "That's probably the understatement of the year," she said and put her head on his shoulder as if they were old lovers.

Or worse, friends.

"My brother, Rafe, is like you," she told him, her fingers dancing over his flesh. "He only talks when it's really important. The strong, silent type, I guess you'd call him. Maybe that's why he's a good photographer. But my sister..." she said, smiling. "Two peas in a pod. I think Carolyn can outtalk even me."

"This I can't imagine."

"It's true. I'm the baby of the family, you see, so believe it or not, I didn't talk until I was three-and-a-half. There was no need for me to say a word, Rafe and Carolyn talked for me. And then one day I just started speaking in full sentences, and I haven't stopped since." She smiled. "So. Your turn...you're an only child," she prodded gently when he didn't speak. "Eddie said so."

"Eddie talked about me?"

"He mentioned you on my first day of work. In fact, Eddie's so young himself, I actually assumed you were just a kid."

"He had me when he was a teenager." Far before he'd finished sowing his wild oats, which had left Reilly alone with his teenage mother, Cheri. But because Eddie hadn't been a cruel kid, just a stupid one without a condom, he'd given them half of the trust fund he'd been born with. Cheri had saved every penny for Reilly's college, which he'd gotten halfway through, studying business and finance, before Eddie decided he wanted back in their lives.

Ten years later, both mother and son were still resisting Eddie's efforts.

"You didn't grow up with him?" Tessa asked.

"No." He could feel her breath against his chest, could feel her waiting for more. "I told you, I'm not good at this."

"Well, we could always escape instead."

She was something, he'd give her that. Determined and spirited and brave as hell. But against him she felt so tiny, and he knew she'd be utterly defenseless in a fight against those four. He traced the bruises on her throat and felt an odd and unwelcoming urge to keep her safe. "It's almost dawn. I'll go soon."

"But—"

He put his finger over her mouth before it could start running again. Had he wanted to protect her? Well, who the hell was going to protect *him*, and not from the perps, but from her? "I said I'd go."

She pulled his hand from her mouth and blinked those dewy eyes up at him. "Okay."

"Why do I get the feeling you don't really mean okay?"

"No, really. I'll...be patient." She shot him a wistful smile. "Just tonight I was wishing for more adventure and excitement in my life. It's why I took the job with your father in the first place. I figured a variety of different tasks at different places would help provide some of that. But now that I've had a real adventure and real excitement, all I want is my own bed, and maybe a bubble bath to go with it."

In spite of himself he smiled. "A bubble bath?"

"Strawberry-scented. What are you wishing for?"

A bottle of something aged and expensive. A faceless woman. A break from the nightmares this night had brought back.

But he'd settle for just being out of here. Alone.

"Reilly?"

What the hell. "Sex."

"*What?*"

"Forget it."

"No, no," she said quickly. "I asked."

Yeah, she'd asked. He lay there on the small cot with her, soaking up the feeling of being so close to another human being, trying not to think of what they could be doing to pass the time.

Maybe silence wasn't the way to go after all, because when her mouth wasn't running off, his other senses sort of took over, starting with how her soft curves felt against him.

"Reilly? What do you do? For a living?"

"Why?"

"Just filling time." She cocked her head. "Is it a secret?"

"Accounting."

"You're an accountant." Her tone was disbelieving.

"Yep."

"What did you do before that?"

"Why?"

Now her lips curved and he couldn't take his eyes off them. Since she was still staring at *his* mouth, he figured it was only fair.

"Is that a secret, too?" she asked.

"Actually, yes."

Her eyes widened. "Really?"

No. He just didn't want to get into it. He didn't like to talk about it, and he wouldn't start now with the woman who was plastered against him from head to toe, feeling soft and sweet and everything he didn't want but suddenly craved.

"It's just that you don't really seem the accountant type to me," she said. "More like...secret agent man or something."

Since that was so close to the truth, he didn't say a word. For distraction, he looked beyond her, out the small window, and saw the pink tinge to the sky. Thank God. "Time," he said, and carefully disentangling himself from her curvy little body, stood.

Tessa stood, too, and watching the enigmatic Reilly Ledger stretching his long, beautiful body, she felt...confused. Several times now she'd actually thought she'd seen a gentler side to this man, it was part of what had made her melt all over him, what had let her allow him to kiss and touch her like he had, and yet then she'd blinked and it had vanished.

It occurred to her how little she really knew about him, other than he had a king-sized alpha attitude. Oh, and that he kissed like heaven.

Good thing she wasn't attracted to attitude, not in the least. Nope, give her a kind, warm, *safe*, beta man any day of the week.

Please give her a kind, warm, safe, beta man. It was her turn for one.

But that kissing like heaven thing...that could be a problem. "You wanted to wait until daylight," she said, trying not to sound as ruffled as she was. "For safety reasons or whatever."

"It's nearly daylight now." He eyed the access above them with the look of someone about to undergo a root canal without drugs.

"You're just trying to get away from me."

He looked so startled, she had to let out a low laugh. "Don't worry. I often have this impact on people, especially..." Her smile faded, and embarrassed at what she'd nearly blurted out, she lifted a shoulder.

"Especially?"

She looked out the window.

"Oh, *now* you're going to go shy on me?"

"On men," she finished. "I often have this impact—that need-to-run impact—on men."

He didn't say anything so she risked a look at him. "What, no comment?"

He was looking at her, his light eyes inscrutable. "I think a guy would be an idiot not to want you. If he was looking for a woman, that is."

"But you're not looking."

He gave a slow shake of his head. "I'm sorry. I'm not looking."

She managed a wobbly smile. "You're very sweet to be so kind about it."

"Sweet and kind are two things I'm most definitely not. Let's get out of here."

"Too much confession going on?"

"Too much something."

She looked out at the brightening dawn. The Angeles Crest Mountains were blooming, as was everything, because in April in Southern California, that's how it went. Just another beautiful day. They were all beautiful days.

Reilly stood on the bed. He was going to get them out and then she'd probably never see him again. Suddenly she couldn't remember what her rush was to get out.

If they got out.

His big, beautiful body was tense, his hands in fists at his sides as he stared up at the access, and despite the utter toughness emanating from him in waves, she once again sensed that there was more, much more to this man. "Reilly—"

"Watch out." He easily reached the ceiling. His arms were taut with strength. Corded tendons stood out in bold relief as he worked the square cover of drywall loose. Under his arms were soft, sparse tufts of dark hair that matched the light spattering across his chest. And those legs...long and delineated with strength. She'd never really understood the debate between boxers and briefs, but the way Reilly filled out his black clingy knit ones made her a firm believer in boxers—

"Tessa?"

"Hmm?" She jerked her gaze off his body, a little horrified to have been caught gawking at the guy who'd been hit on the head, stripped and was now doing his damnedest to get them out of their hell.

His disconcerted gaze told her he knew exactly what she'd been doing and that he hadn't found it so flattering. He had the drywall off and was handing it down to her.

She took it, set it against the wall and turned back in time to see him pulling himself up with the agility of an athlete. His head and chest disappeared, leaving just the bottom half—which was not a bad view at all—and then he was gone entirely.

A flash of panic hit her, but then he poked his head back in. "I'll be back for you."

"No." She'd gone all shaky again at the thought of being there alone. Before she could think, she leaped onto the cot and reached her hands up. "Take me with you."

There was a conflicted look on his chiseled features. "I'll be right back, Tess."

"No. Don't leave me here alone. *Please?*" She lifted her arms up toward him, knowing the impossibility of him being able to pull her up, but—

But nothing. With a grim expression, he reached down, grabbed her hand and pulled her up into the opening of the attic with such ease she could hardly believe it. He scooted back to make room for her as she sat on a beam, surrounded by more beams and insulation.

Yep, they were in the attic, which gaped open to large and unknown depths. In the darkness she could see nothing but Reilly, and had no idea how she'd imagined this as a great plan. "It's...dark."

"Yeah." Hunched over his knees, he rubbed his hands over his face. "I thought for a moment there you'd been shocked into silence."

"And you liked it, right?" She rolled her eyes and mimicked zipping her lips and tossing away the key.

"Don't tease me," he said, and looked around. "Okay, listen. I want you to follow me. And seriously, toss away that key. We have no idea if we're alone and once we get over another access, any noise at all will echo down."

"I'll be quiet. Let's just do this."

"Right." He turned away from her and looked into the black, dusty gloom of the gaping attic.

And didn't move.

"Reilly?"

"Yeah."

But he still didn't budge. She touched his bare shoulder. Beneath her fingers, his muscles leaped. "Hey. You okay?"

"Terrific. I love being in a small enclosed space with no light."

"You're really afraid of the dark?"

He didn't look at her.

"Or...claustrophobic?"

"Neither, exactly." His eyes glittered with humiliation and a good amount of bad temper. "I just had a bad experience and..."

"Oh, Reilly." Leaning in, she hugged him. She couldn't help it, because realizing that this big, bad, brooding man was really just a soft and squishy beta on the inside was the most attractive thing about him. And given the outer package, that was saying something.

But he set her away from him with just enough barely restrained roughness to tell her she'd poked at the hungry lion one too many times. "Let's move it."

"You should have just boosted me up here," she said, trying to soothe. "I could have—"

"I thought you threw away the key to your mouth."

Okay, so she'd only imagined his soft spot.

Without looking back to see her roll her eyes again, he moved forward. "And stay on the beam," he commanded softly.

She followed, watching the lines of his sleek, smooth back, the way the black knit boxers hugged his tight butt and thighs, trying to convince herself she was so over her momentary lapse into lustville. So over him, period.

THE ATTIC WAS PITCH-BLACK except for where the occasional vent to the outside allowed slats of light to shoot in. Grateful for any light no matter how meager, Reilly stopped and bent as close as he could to the first access panel they came across, only to hear a muffled thump from below. Not a good sign. "Does my father have a daily maid service?"

Tessa came up behind him and put her hand low on his spine as she tried to see around him.

He felt his muscles leap at the touch and knew she'd felt it, too, when she skimmed her hand up and down his bare flesh as if soothing him.

He wondered what she'd do if she discovered that her touch was doing the opposite of soothing. "Does he?"

"I don't know." She set her chin on his shoulder as she whispered into his ear.

Her hair tickled his nose and smelled like a bunch of flowers. "Give me some room," he muttered, and shrugged her off. Now he was distracted again, damn it, with thoughts of stupid flowers and all the bedrooms—empty—that his father had in this house and the things they could do in those empty bedrooms—

"Reilly."

He sighed and glanced over his shoulder.

The lines of light slashed across her features. Her eyes were as big as saucers. "I hear voices," she said a little shakily. "And they're not maids. Not unless Eddie has hired big thugs who like to choke and throw women."

Ah, hell. He squeezed her hand. "Tess…"

"Why would they still be there?" She sounded a little less thrilled about their great escape now. "They could have cleaned the place out and been far gone by now if they'd wanted."

He'd been wondering the same thing. "Did you happen to mention to the guy who grabbed you that Eddie wouldn't be back for a few days?"

"Of course n—" She bit her lip and looked stricken. "Oh."

"Oh, what?"

"I guess I might have said something when I was arguing with him."

Wasn't that just perfect?

"I'm sorry."

Another thump, a closer one now.

Turning to her, he slid his hand across her mouth and put his lips to her ear. "Shh."

When she nodded, he removed his hand but stared at her for a long time. Her hair was wild, and so were her eyes. He couldn't see the bruises one of the assholes below had left on her but knew they were still there. And though he couldn't see her thoughts, she felt icy cold, and was trembling, her terror coming through loud and clear.

He squeezed her gently, trying to get some of his warmth into her. Ironic that he was sweating from being enclosed and she was a virtual Popsicle. "I want you to go back," he said in her ear. "Go back to where we climbed up and wait there—"

She gripped him tight. "No—"

"I'm going to go alone. I can do it silently—"

"So can I—"

"No." He didn't want to bet on that, as he doubted she'd ever done anything silently in her entire life. "I'm going to drop down into the farthest room I can get to and then—"

"What if they find you?"

"They won't."

If he'd thought her eyes were big before, they were huge now, though he couldn't see her exact expression. "You're afraid of the dark, but you'll take on four armed men?" she asked incredulously.

He felt the muscle in his jaw start jumping again. "I've had worse odds."

"What did you say you did before you were an accountant?"

"Go back. Go back now."

"You were on the right side of legal though, right? You *are* the good guy, *right?*"

"Go." He nudged her to turn around.

"But—" She fought him and turned to face him again, all the while maintaining her balance on the beam.

He was beginning to see how she'd gotten herself so roughed up last night. But when he felt the fear coming off her in waves, he gave her one last squeeze. "Look, I'm coming right back for you," he promised, although he never made promises. "Go, Tess."

Then he physically turned her away from him once more, and gave her a little shove. This involved putting his hands on her and shockingly, he wanted to linger. Soothe. Calm.

Wasn't that the damnedest thing.

But to do what he had to do, he put her firmly out of his mind with one deep breath. Despite being starving and half naked, he now concentrated on the task at hand.

That being not getting his ass kicked again.

5

WHEN TESSA KNEW A BETTER WAY, she wasn't particularly good at following directions. She tried though, she really did. She understood Reilly wanted her out of the way so he wouldn't have to worry about her as he dropped down into the house and tried to get them out safely.

She got that.

And she knew she'd never forget the sight of him forging ahead. Not afraid or uneasy—except for his aversion to the dark. Nope, no holding back for this man. And he hadn't simply crawled along either.

He'd prowled. Like an animal on the hunt.

It occurred to her, and not for the first time, that under certain circumstances Reilly Ledger could be a dangerous man. Which, really, would only matter to her if she was attracted to him.

Damn it, she was attracted to him. That in turn was as unsettling as the sound of something scurrying off in the darkness.

Probably just a mouse, but she had a general thing against mice. Even so, she made it all the way back to the attic access above the room in which they'd spent the night. Huddling at the opening, arms wrapped around her knees, she looked down at the cot where they'd slept together, and that's where she went wrong.

She started thinking.

Too much.

She started obsessing over what could be happening to Reilly right at that very moment. Clearly the guy thought he was invincible. He thought he could handle anything.

But despite his tough attitude, he was just an accountant. What if he didn't make it? What then? What if they caught him and killed him this time?

No, she told herself when she started to shake. Reilly could take care of himself. She'd never met anyone more capable of taking care of himself.

After all, he'd had a gun. *What kind of accountant carries a gun?*

Don't be the stupid chick, she reminded herself. Just climb back down into the room and huddle in a corner and be a good girl.

She had just hooked a leg over the opening when a sound from below stopped her cold. Her heart took off racing as she went as still as she could while shaking like a leaf, but it was no good. With her blood roaring through her ears she couldn't hear.

What if someone was down there waiting for her?

Suddenly, the stupid chick idea of going back to Reilly seemed like the *smart* chick idea.

Once the decision was made, she carefully turned around, but still managed to move too quickly and lost a shoe. She watched it fall into the gray room and gave a sort of fatalistic shrug. In the scheme of things, if all she lost was a shoe, she'd feel pretty darn lucky.

Crawling back wasn't as easy alone. She religiously followed the exact path they'd taken earlier, only this time without her six-foot human shield, removing the cobwebs that she felt certain held big, hairy spiders. She tried not to think about that, tried to think of other things...such as what could be happening to Reilly at this very moment.

She crawled faster. When she got halfway, she paused to listen for clues, but silence reigned. As quietly as she could and holding her breath, she continued past the point where she'd left Reilly. She could see another access panel up ahead, but still couldn't hear a single sign of life. When she got to it, she could see this was where Reilly had dropped down. He'd muscled off the cover and left a gaping hole revealing what looked like a pristine tiled guest bathroom.

Speaking of which, after a long night, she needed one badly. Stomach growling as well, she carefully lowered her head into the opening. Yep, a bathroom. She reversed her position and stuck her feet through, thinking if she could just keep a good hold on the edge, she could lower herself down the entire length of her body, and hopefully reduce her fall by a full five feet, three inches.

Okay, five feet two.

She slid through, her dress snagging up around her hips as she hung there by her fingers, praying she really was the only one in the room, otherwise she was presenting quite the picture.

She took one last peek over her shoulder, and had just enough time to realize it was still a long fall when her fingers gave way.

She crumpled to the floor with a crash-landing that wasn't the quiet one she'd hoped for. Quick as she could, she leaped to her feet and took a quick inventory.

No broken bones, just a sore butt. Good thing for her extra padding then. She was still missing a shoe, but she could live with that. Because she had to, she made use of the facilities, and then looked around her for something, anything, to use to protect herself. Silver tile, silver towels with gold bows, silver gilt around the mirrors and a bar of silver soap in the shape of a seashell. She needed...ah-ha. On the back of the toilet, she grabbed up one of two long silver candlestick holders, tossing aside the pretty ivory candle.

She hefted the thing in her hand like a weapon and was gratified by the weight.

What she wasn't gratified by was the sick pit in her stomach. How many times had her big brother tried to teach her self-defense? How many times had she ended up on the mat laughing with Rafe shaking his head in disgust. She wasn't laughing now, and with all her might she wished he was here.

Tiptoeing to the door, she cracked it open and peeked out. Nothing. She stepped out of the bathroom, brandishing the candlestick out in front of her as if she knew what she was doing.

Up ahead, she could see the vast living room, and beyond that, the kitchen. Then she caught a flash of movement in there and plastered herself against the wall, nearly hyperventilating.

With her pulse at a full marathon rate, she scooted her way down the hallway to the opening of the living room. No one. She moved toward the sliding glass door.

On the other side, in the kitchen before the island, facing away from her, Reilly suddenly appeared. Then he bent down, momentarily disappearing from her view, and when he came up again, there was a gun in his hand.

An involuntary gasp escaped her, and gun out, he whirled. For one dizzy moment all she could see was the muzzle pointed right at her. Before she could blink, he'd uncocked it, or whatever one did when one didn't intend to shoot after all, and was standing before her, jerking her out of the living room, into the kitchen and around the corner. His laser beam eyes demanded answers but when she opened her mouth he put a hand to it, just as her thug came around the corner, still wearing his jeans and dirty thermal shirt.

When he saw them he raised an arm with a knife.

Reilly shoved her down and kicked the knife out of the guy's hands with chilling ease, adding another well-placed kick to his stomach.

The guy doubled over, then fell to his knees, mouth opening and closing like a fish out of water before he flopped all the way to the floor.

Reilly stood over him. "What are you after?"

The guy offered a snide but interesting suggestion on what Reilly could do to himself. Reilly grabbed him by the hair and calmly lifted, then let his head hit the floor.

Given the squeal of pain this invoked, it was a hard hit.

"*What are you after?*" Reilly asked again.

"We were just going to mess up the place, that's all."

"Why?"

The guy apparently hesitated too long for the impatient Reilly, and got another head bump on the floor.

"Ouch! Stop!"

"Then talk."

"Okay, look, we were hired to steal his stuff and mess the place up, *that's all.*"

Reilly looked unimpressed. "Keep talking."

"But we just thought since he was going to be gone, we'd camp out and live here for a few days. You know, really trash it in style."

"Who's paying you?"

He closed his eyes. "I don't know."

Reilly stood up. The guy on the floor kicked out to trip him.

Tessa cried out a warning and huddled back against the wall, but Reilly didn't need her help. He did some sort of karate chop to the guy's throat and out he went like a light.

There was a coil of rope on the counter and a knife. "Where did those come from?" she whispered.

"From our captors." Reilly efficiently and quickly tied him up, and when he was done, he nodded curtly to Tessa. "Nice to know you can follow directions."

"I..." Stunned by what she'd just seen, she just stared at him.

He gave her that long-suffering sigh she seemed to cause. "Call it in."

"What?"

"I got all four of them," he said with that eerie calm knack for understating. "Call 9-1-1."

She started to stand but her knees were knocking together. From her perch on the cold tile floor she could see the other side of the island now, where two men lay bound and gagged.

"The fourth is in the foyer, also prone." He moved back into the kitchen and picked up the phone on the wall, then shook his head with disgust. "They cut the lines. Come on—"

He grabbed her hand and pulled her up. For a moment, one very weak moment, she let her hands come to rest on his bare pecs but she resisted the urge to put her head down and beg for comfort because she'd just realized something more than a little unsettling.

Reilly Ledger was not hiding himself behind his tough, rough, dangerously edgy exterior. He *was* that tough, rough, dangerously edgy exterior.

Standing there, with the bad guys at his feet, he glanced around. Coolly. "Need my cell phone," he said. "*Stay.*" He left for a moment, and came back with an armful of clothes that he dropped and started to pull on. A black T-shirt. Black jeans, from which he took out a cell phone and called 9-1-1 while he slid his feet into black athletic shoes.

As he talked to dispatch, he shoved his gun—the one he'd retrieved from one of the men on the floor—into his waistband. She tried not to think about that, that he carried a weapon on him, but she could do little else. She heard a half-hysterical giggle and was surprised to find it had come from her.

"Hey." He clicked off the phone and looked at her, now fully dressed.

How was it he looked even more devastatingly dangerous fully dressed?

"You okay?"

A question from the man so miserly with words. She started to nod her head, then slowly shook it instead. Overwhelmed by the entire night's events, by his utter calmness, by everything, she did as she'd wanted to moments ago. She set her head on his chest and hung on for all she was worth.

"Tess—"

She lifted her head. "I'm sorry. I just need…" Their mouths were a fraction of an inch apart. God, he was gorgeous. She was sure he'd hate that, but— "I really need a hug."

His arms encircled her.

"Thank you," she whispered, something warm and gushy happening to her insides at his touch. He did that for her, made her feel so secure that she could move on from the fright.

And move on she did. What was it that made her so suddenly, ridiculously turned-on? The danger? The shocking violence Reilly had just displayed? There had to be something sick in that, she decided, but it didn't take away from the fact that her nipples had hardened and her thighs tightened.

Maybe it was the embrace itself. Or maybe it was simply Reilly's presence, or the fact that she already knew how good he kissed, how delicious his touch was, but being with him made her feel…she glanced at the restrained bad guys…safe.

It was true. Reilly, for all his brooding intensity, made her feel safe, so she had no idea, no idea at all, why she shivered.

His arms tightened around her. Mouth still so close to hers she could feel his warm breath, he said, "Don't go into shock now."

"No."

His eyes roamed her face, settling on her lips. His

arms were banded tightly around her. "You're still shaking."

"I think…I think the adrenaline is getting to me."

"What do you mean?"

"I think…I want you. I want you a lot."

With a groan, his eyes became slumberous and…hot, definitely hot. "Tess—" One large hand palmed the back of her head and he slowly changed the angle of his head. Their noses brushed, but not their lips, not quite. Feeling a little desperate, a little like this was her last shot because the police were coming and then it'd be over, she closed the slight gap between them and laid one on him.

She expected to have to coax him out of his contained, tight control, as she had last time, but his mouth opened to hers immediately, and he fed her a hot kiss, holding her to him as if she was the very air he required. He was certainly hers. She lost herself in the sounds of their ravaging kiss, in the feel of his hands running up and down her back, squeezing her bottom, gliding her against the enticing bulge now firmly behind the buttons on his Levi's.

Don't stop, was her only coherent thought, and as if he'd heard her, he turned, pressing her against the wall, protecting her from view of any of the men bound on the floor. He slid his hand over her breast. His fingers teased her nipple and the sensation dissolved her bones. But then he pulled his mouth back slightly, breathing harder than when he'd fought the bad guys.

She'd done that to him, and the power that knowledge infused her with was shocking. "That...that was some adrenaline rush."

Another pass of his thumb over her nipple. "Yeah."

She would have slid to the floor if he hadn't been holding her up. She needed a bucket of ice water, something to bring back her temporarily vacationing sanity—

The sound of a siren coming closer did just the trick.

THE SUN FULLY ROSE as they all stood on Eddie's driveway. In the bright L.A. sunshine, surrounded by officers, Reilly answered all the questions he could. Yes, he was Eddie Ledger's son. Yes, Eddie had known he'd be coming by, because he'd left Reilly a note—one of many in the past ten years since he'd decided he wanted back in his son's life. No, the note hadn't specifically said to come by last night, just that he'd wanted to talk.

Eddie always wanted to talk these days. The man had grown up, just ask him and he'd be happy to tell you. He'd also be happy to tell you that Reilly needed to accept that they were a family, father and son. To prove it, he was constantly barging into his son's world with a wide smile and a full wallet, because he wasn't picky—he'd buy his way into Reilly's affections if he had to. He wanted Reilly to come to watch the Lakers with him, he wanted Reilly to hop on a plane to Barbados with him, he wanted…so much Reilly had no idea how to take it.

He'd compromised, accepting temp office workers from Eddie's vast and surprisingly talented working pool when his office manager needed the extra help, which she usually did. But up until now, that had been about the extent of it.

So, no, he told the officer, he didn't know Eddie's regular habits enough to know if the burglars had been watching him. He didn't know Eddie's enemies—only that given his various corporations and their successes, he was sure to have them. And, no, he didn't know why Eddie had sent him a note if he was going to be out of town. As he said, when it came to his father's life, he knew very little.

The police hauled the four perps out of the house and into the backs of two different squad cars.

Tessa was being questioned, too, by a woman cop, and was nodding vigorously. Then she pointed at Reilly, and followed it with a look that changed considerably when she saw him looking right back at her. She went from cool and calm to flustered and blushing.

She could have been thinking any number of things, but he figured there were two things in particular that might put that look on her face.

Two kisses.

He'd lost it with her, and if he was being honest, which he nearly always was, it had been more than just the lip-locking. Somewhere in the dark of the night he'd shown her a little something of himself, something he liked to keep hidden.

One thing his work had always shown him, first in the military and then in the CIA, was how important it was to keep the real Reilly deep within where no one could touch him; not a commanding officer, not the enemy, no one.

Tessa, whether she knew it or not, had seen glimpses of the man he hadn't shown anyone in years. If ever. Sure, he'd hugged and kissed and touched more than his share of women, but none as innocently as he just had with her. And none had left him in the morning with this vague uneasy knowledge that he'd like more.

Wrong place, wrong time, wrong woman.

Well, maybe wrong place, wrong time, but he couldn't help feeling she was right. Which is why he needed the hell out.

She was looking at him again and still talking. What the hell did the woman have to say that it could possibly take so long? Her eyes were shuttered a bit as she spoke now, watching him watch her. Shuttered and a bit wary.

Maybe she was no more thrilled than he was to have this face-to-face in-the-light-of-day thing. In fact, she looked downright embarrassed.

Because of what they'd done? Because of what, for one night, they'd been to each other? They could just go their own separate ways, and forget all about this last long night from hell. He'd go to his office, and she'd go to...wherever she belonged.

And that was a good thing, a very good thing.

WHEN REILLY FINALLY got home, to the house on the top of the bluff in South Pasadena where he could see for miles and miles and no one could see him, he stripped—all the way to the skin this time. He took a long, hot shower, ate, and then headed for bed, hitting play on his message machine as he did.

"Reilly."

Naked, Reilly stopped in the middle of his bedroom and looked at the machine.

"Just had a call from the cops."

His father, of course. How like him not to bother to identify himself.

"Christ, did they really wreck the place? I hope you managed to save my Beemer, and that they didn't take her out for any joyrides," Eddie said, laughing softly.

That was Eddie. Everything was all one big joke, including life.

"Anyway...I hear you took care of Tessa. She's special, isn't she? Such a sweet kid."

Reilly would give her the sweet part. Sweet and...hot. He was still scorching from their last connection.

But kid? He had no idea how he'd ever thought it.

"I'm glad you were there for her."

Would Eddie still be so glad if he'd seen how Reilly

had nearly devoured her in the servant's bed? Or how about in the kitchen, pressed there against the wall with his hand up her shirt? Just the thought of that little scene revved his exhausted engines all over again. If the police hadn't come when they had—

"She's the best temp I have," Eddie continued. "Anyway, I'm coming home early, tomorrow morning."

Well, wonders never cease, Eddie was actually going to take this seriously enough to cut short something fun. Amazing.

"Anyway, son, I just wanted to thank you."

Reilly didn't want to be thanked. He wanted to be left alone.

"Means a lot, that you took care of me like that," Eddie said into the room.

Yeah, like you always took care of me? Reilly lay on his bed and studied his open-beamed ceiling, wishing he'd turned the volume off on the machine. "I didn't do it for you," he said to the phone, as if Eddie could hear him.

"I'm just glad you were there. She's one of my favorite employees."

If that wasn't a load of crap. They both knew damn well that as long as the employees were female, they were all Eddie's favorites.

"Call me. You know my cell."

Reilly closed his eyes. He meant to drift off, he'd long ago taught himself to clear his mind and sleep at will.

Only today his mind wouldn't clear and sleep evaded him.

Instead, he pictured mossy wet eyes and lips that tasted like heaven—when they were kissing him, that is, and not talking.

6

TESSA WENT HOME to her little apartment, trying not to think. She didn't want to remember facing those burglars and she didn't want to remember meeting Reilly. And she really didn't want to remember what she'd done with him, because to have lusted like that so quickly, so...fiery, was just damn uncomfortable in the light of day.

Being just outside downtown Los Angeles, she had a lovely view of the city line, complete with smog to the south and the Angeles Crest Mountains to the north.

She parked beneath the carport and felt smug about getting a covered spot—normally she was forced to park in the blazing hot sun. But normally she wasn't coming home at ten in the morning on a Saturday either.

She got out of her VW but instead of seeing her place, she saw Eddie's. She remembered how Reilly had looked standing outside the house, his dark hair gleaming beneath the sunrise, his face not giving away much of anything. He'd stood there with easy confidence and a relaxed air, even though she knew damn well he wasn't relaxed.

They hadn't said goodbye.

Her building was red brick with white trim, and being mid-spring, the small yard was out in full bloom. Since her sister, Carolyn, who was in charge of the landscaping for the place, hadn't yet mowed, Tessa sank in up to her ankles as she crossed the small lawn to her front door. Two-B, home sweet home, where there were no nasty-tempered burglars, no guns, no small gray cots and no tall, dark and wildly magnificent strangers who kissed so well she lost brain cells every time she thought about it.

She sighed and fished through her purse for her keys. Everything seemed so normal here, so quiet, it was hard to believe what the last twenty-four hours had held.

Her sister popped out of apartment One-B so fast Tessa dropped her keys.

"So did you forget my phone number?" Carolyn asked very politely, tossing back her long, dark-blond hair.

Oh boy, the queen of the Delacantro household was ticked. "No, I didn't forget your phone number."

Eyes that matched her own flashed at her and Tessa sighed. Carolyn thought of Tessa as her little chick, and she really hated it when her little chick didn't toe the line. "Then maybe you got swept off your feet by a wild hunk of a man who held you prisoner all night long," she suggested. "Maybe that's why you didn't call me to join you at your boss's fancy house."

A half-hysterical laugh bubbled out of Tessa. "You know, that's just close enough to the truth to be scary. Except—" She opened her apartment door, not surprised when her sister followed her inside.

Her sister always came in uninvited, ate her ice cream uninvited, felt obligated to tell Tessa she was wrong on a regular basis uninvited...and Tessa loved her anyway.

She tossed her purse and keys into the wicker basket on the floor where she put everything she didn't want to lose, sank to her couch, and sighed in pleasure. God, it felt like it'd been a year since she'd been home.

"Except...what?" her sister asked.

"Well, while he *was* a rather wild hunk, he didn't hold me prisoner all night long. Four other guys did that."

Carolyn laughed.

Tessa didn't.

And slowly Carolyn's smile faded. She eyed Tessa's sundress, a bit dusty from her crawl through Eddie's attic. "You wore that yesterday."

"Yep."

"You never repeat clothes."

"Nope."

"Tessa...where's your left shoe?"

"Oh. I forgot to go back for it." Her apartment consisted of the "great" room—kitchen, living room and dining room all in one—and a small bedroom and bathroom. Since she favored bright colors, the place was full of them, from the blue-and-green couch she sat on to the sunshine-yellow kitchen table and matching chairs she'd painted herself, to the plants she had thriving in every corner. On the walls were Rafe's photographs—some abstract, some of their family, some of the places he'd traveled to far and wide. She sank deeper into the couch, kicked off her one shoe and put her feet up. "I'm starving."

Carolyn was still staring at her. Slowly she came to the couch, hunkered down near Tessa and took her hand. "Honey, you're scaring me."

"I know how you feel about cooking, but I swear I'll be your best friend if you could whip me up some toast and an egg or something. Even PB and J would be great."

Carolyn didn't budge. "Are you hurt?"

"Do I look hurt?"

"Your dress has a tear—" She fingered a rip at the seam over Tessa's collarbone. Then her eyes went hot, and she reached out and touched Tessa's throat. Her extremely bruised throat. "Oh my God. Baby, you're—"

"It's okay."

"I'm calling the police."

Tessa caught her hand and brought it up to her cheek, turning her face into it. "I'm okay."

With her other hand, Carolyn stroked Tessa's hair off her face. "Are you sure? What happened? Tell me everything."

"This is the worst of it," she said of the bruises. "I promise."

"So you weren't—"

"No one touched me." Well, no one that she hadn't wanted to.

"Spill, damn it. Tell me right now or I'm calling Rafe."

Their brother was the oldest of the three of them and even more protective than Carolyn. When his sisters had first started dating, it'd nearly killed him. Eventually, he'd gotten used to it, but only by pretending they were still virgins.

If Rafe thought she'd been hurt, nothing would stop him from exacting revenge. "I was supposed to watch Eddie's house this weekend."

"Yes," her sister said impatiently. "The boss's house in the La Canada hills with all its riches and finery. What happened, Tessa?"

"When I let myself in, I interrupted a burglary in progress."

Carolyn's mouth fell open. "Oh my God."

"Before I could get out of the house, one of them grabbed me and locked me in a room so he could finish what he'd started, which was stealing from Eddie."

Carolyn wrapped her arms around Tessa. "He grabbed you?"

"Luckily, all he wanted was me out of his way. Eddie's son had also been shoved into this room, so I wasn't alone."

"Eddie has a son? Is he okay?"

"He's not a little kid, he's...all grown up." *Really* grown up.

"So the two of you were together, locked in a room? All night long?"

She tried not to squirm because Carolyn could read a squirm at thirty miles. "Yes."

"Tell me he's a nice guy, Tessa."

Her sister looked so distraught, so worried, she managed a smile. And though "nice" wasn't quite the word she would have used to describe Reilly Ledger, she said, "He's a very nice guy."

Her sister studied her for a long moment. "You must have been terrified."

How to explain that with Reilly her terror had taken a back seat to other things, such as a lust she was embarrassed about now.

"How did you get out?"

Good. A question she could answer. "We waited for dawn, then crawled up through an attic access. Eddie's son beat the crap out of the bad guys and called the cops."

Carolyn's eyes were huge. "Does Eddie's son have a name?"

"Reilly."

"And he was good to you."

"Very," she said simply.

"Well, then." Carolyn squeezed Tessa again. "I want to hug him, too."

"He's not really the huggable type." She hugged her sister back because, now that it was over, things other than fear were beginning to make themselves known. Embarrassment, exhaustion, hunger... "You know what I really want?"

"What, baby?" said Carolyn, stroking her hair. "Anything. You want me to go burn something for you?"

Tessa let out a little laugh and burrowed in closer. "Yes. But while you do that, I want a long, hot shower. I'm going to go wash it all out of my system." She pulled free and headed toward her bedroom. "Lots of butter on the toast, okay? And can you try to scramble an egg? I have cheese you could add to it—"

"I'll get it."

"Thank you," she whispered, a little too close to tears. All her life she'd fought her two siblings for her independence, for liberation from "baby" status, but at the moment, she felt just shaky enough to be grateful for the way they loved to smother her.

As she stripped and stepped into the steam and hot water, nearly whimpering in gratitude at how it felt on her bruised, tired body, she wondered what Reilly was doing right now.

The man had a serious back-off attitude. She sincerely doubted he'd ever let anyone baby and comfort him... So where was he now? All alone? Shaken? Needing to be consoled and reassured?

Lonely?

Then she laughed at herself. She had a feeling that the man enjoyed being alone, very much. He wouldn't ever be weak enough to need someone to comfort him.

And he sure as hell didn't seem the type to need to be reassured about anything.

A knock came on the bathroom door, just before it opened. "I brought you some hot tea," Carolyn said.

"Thanks." Hot tea. She should want that and her bed. But she didn't think she'd be able to sleep with her mind whirling around in circles the way it was.

"I'll just leave it here on the counter," her sister said over the rush of the water. "You doing okay?"

"Sure."

"Are you almost done?"

Tessa sighed and stuck her head out of the shower curtain. "You called him, didn't you."

Carolyn held out Tessa's portable phone.

Tessa turned off the water and put the phone in the crook of her neck. "Hey, big brother."

"Tell me you're really okay."

At the sound of Rafe's voice, low and rough with concern, her throat went tight. "I'm really okay."

But her voice cracked and he swore softly. "Tessa, listen. I'm in Paris on a photo shoot but I'll get on the next plane—"

"No." She both laughed and sobbed and wiped her nose. "I'm fine, I promise."

"You don't sound fine."

"It's your voice. That's all," she said. "I heard you

and...I miss you. But I'm not hurt, I'm just tired and hungry."

"You're always hungry."

"Yes, so you know I must be okay, right?"

Rafe sighed. "Promise me. Promise me you're not lying just so I won't come home early."

"I promise."

"I'm going to call you tonight."

"And probably every day until you come home," Tessa teased, somehow feeling better just for talking to the brother who'd spent a lifetime making her feel better.

"You know it," he said. "And Tessa? You also know Carolyn's going to be hovering."

"Doesn't she always?" They both laughed over that for a moment, then Rafe got serious. "Take care of yourself. I'll see you soon. And when I do, I want to meet this guy who helped you."

"Love you," Tessa said, avoiding the subject of Reilly, and when she clicked off, she tried to find the peace the shower had given her, but the thought of Reilly had shattered it.

He kissed like heaven.

That thought came out of nowhere, and as Carolyn left the bathroom, Tessa went still in the act of drying off, having conveniently and completely blanked that part out of her recollection of the events to her sister.

She'd instigated the kiss. The *kisses*. She'd practically begged him for them. That he'd caved in spite of trying to be hard and edgy and distant was of little consolation now.

She hated that she'd gone weak and girly on him, that she'd needed comfort in the first place, but bottom line...it had happened and she couldn't change it. So it was probably for the best that they'd each gone their separate ways after the police had arrived, without speaking again.

Sighing, she tossed aside her towel and prepared to go on with her life, secure in the knowledge she could make it through anything, including being held hostage.

Including being kissed and touched by a man she'd inexplicably been drawn to in the face of danger; a wild, tough kind of man she'd never see again.

Which was just as well, really. She was quite certain in the light of a normal day she'd never be attracted to a man like Reilly Ledger. Never.

REILLY GOT UP EARLY on Sunday morning. He ran his usual five miles. Showered and grabbed a quick breakfast.

Alone. The way he liked it.

Alone was easy. Alone meant not needing to worry about anyone but himself. Alone meant doing as he pleased, when he pleased.

Alone was...habit.

He knew what that said about him. At least he knew what his mother thought that said about him. He sure as hell knew what the women in his life thought that said about him—they'd all been clear as crystal on their way out his door.

He was selfish.

He didn't feel.

He was a robot.

Then there'd been the woman who'd simply tried to kill him. That was a memory for the books and had a great deal to do with his dislike of close, dark places, but he wasn't going to go there.

And yes, maybe he *was* a little selfish, but he sure as hell *felt* things, far more than he liked. As for being a robot, well, would a robot have responded to Tessa's soft, giving body and hungry mouth?

Not likely.

Okay, settled then. He spent the rest of his weekend in precious solitude. And if he occasionally thought about Tessa, wondered how she was coping with the memory of the ordeal, he told himself it was out of general concern. The way he'd be concerned about anyone who'd faced such a trauma.

It was nothing personal. He just knew personal trauma, that's all.

So why he dreamed so vividly at night—dark, haunting dreams that he couldn't quite remember in the morning—was beyond him.

Or maybe he just didn't want to remember.

His father called and again thanked him for helping Tessa but, looking back, Reilly couldn't say that he'd helped her all that much. Everything he'd done had been for himself—climbing through the attic, nailing his captors...kissing Tess. That had definitely been for him. At the time she'd overwhelmed his body and senses. He supposed he should be glad it hadn't gone any further, as that would have been even more difficult to face now.

And things were pretty difficult as they were.

MONDAY MORNING DAWNED bright and clear. Just as Reilly was leaving for work, he heard a knock at his door. He grabbed the leather saddlebag he used as a briefcase, figuring he'd turn down whomever was trying to sell him something on his way out.

Eddie stood there—tall, lean, fit, looking much younger than his forty-nine years. His dark hair was in artful disarray, his clothes no doubt picked out by a stylist. His smile was genuine and made Reilly groan.

"Morning, son." Eddie lifted a McDonald's bag, which they both knew damn well was a bribe.

A bribe Reilly was willing to take if there was a breakfast sandwich in there.

"I have tickets to the ball game tonight. Join me?"

Reilly took his gaze off the bag. "Just you?"

"Well, I thought I'd invite a few friends along."

Women. Not that Reilly had a problem with women, but Eddie always overdid a good time. There'd be a horde of them and Reilly didn't like hordes.

A loud honk came from the driveway. Reilly popped

his head out the door and saw Eddie's red convertible BMW, filled to capacity.

With women.

In this case, given the size of the car, that meant *three* women. "Small harem today," Reilly noted. "You really need a bigger car."

Eddie sighed. "I keep telling you I've changed. I like them one at a time these days."

"Or three."

"Reilly—"

"Look, it's your life."

"Yeah, you keep saying that." For a moment, frustration swam in Eddie's eyes. "But I want you in that life, damn it."

"I'm in it. How can I help it, you keep showing up on my doorstep."

Eddie sighed again, then let out a rough laugh. "I keep hoping that one of these days you'll show up on mine."

"You've got a pretty full plate at the moment." Reilly nodded toward the carload, which reminded him of his biggest life's goal—*Don't turn out like good old Dad.*

"Those are my employees, son."

Reilly opened the McDonald's bag. The delicious scent of fast-food wafted up. "Didn't anyone ever tell you not to mix business with pleasure?"

"No. No one ever told me anything of the sort. I learned the hard way."

Reilly had heard Eddie's poor-little-rich-boy story

before, how his parents had ignored him all his life for their travels, etc. It didn't wash. Reilly hadn't had a father around either, until lately anyway, and no one caught him whining about it.

"And give me some credit for growing up, would you?" Eddie grinned sheepishly. "Better late than never, right?" When Reilly didn't crack a smile in return, he sighed again. "The women out there really are my employees. I'm taking two of them into my real estate division today, we're shorthanded. Totally on the up-and-up. The other is a woman I thought you'd recognize."

Reilly took another look. The woman in the front passenger seat wore sunglasses covering what he knew to be mossy-green eyes that showed her every emotion as soon as she thought it. Her hair was tucked behind her ears, emphasizing her face, which he knew to be soft to the touch.

For one beat their gazes collided and Reilly stood there, inexplicably riveted.

Tessa looked away first.

"Her car wouldn't start this morning," Eddie said. "I offered her a ride to her temp job."

"She's working today?"

"She's one tough cookie." Eddie blocked Reilly's view of her and dropped the smile. "She insisted on coming in. I don't know if it's because she needs the money or if she needs to keep busy."

Ah, hell. He didn't want to know this. Aware that he

was letting his guard slip, he peered around Eddie. She sat very still, staring straight forward now. "Is this job an easy one?"

Eddie paused so long Reilly took his gaze off Tessa to his father. "Is it?"

Eddie stared at him, then looked away. "No. But I have a feeling she's going to be all right."

It was true. She was bright, brave and adventurous. She'd be all right.

"Enjoy the food, son." Reilly stepped off the porch. "Oh, and I have you on the calendar for a temp through Thursday. Is that right?"

"Yeah." His business was up and down, up at the moment. His office manager did most of the everyday work. She'd been after him to hire another permanent office staff member, but Reilly wasn't ready for permanent.

"Want her with the usual prerequisites? Old and grumpy?"

"Funny."

"Oh, come on, admit it," Eddie said. "You like old and grumpy."

"I like experienced."

"Well, so do I, son. So do I. I'll see you." He started to walk away. "Oh, and live a little today, why don't you. Just for fun."

When Eddie drove off, Reilly locked his front door and headed down his steps. He'd like to say he forgot all about his father and the women in the BMW, specifically the one woman in the front seat. After all, he was good about forgetting things that got to him.

And there was no doubt, Tessa Delacantro had gotten to him.

The last time he'd let a woman do that, he'd ended up on the wrong side of a beating he'd like to forget, both physically and mentally.

He sure was melancholy today. Flipping on his sunglasses, he slid behind the wheel of his car, cranked up the Metallica CD and drove.

By the time he got to work, he felt better. The food had helped, so had Metallica. Nothing like heavy metal to clear one's head. His building was in San Marino, a small, exclusive suburb of Los Angeles, where he took up the fifth floor of a small glass-and-brick building overlooking the San Gabriel Mountains to the north and the San Gabriel Valley to the south. To the west lay downtown Los Angeles and its famous skyline, highlighted nicely today by a ring of smog. He didn't mind the smog because he loved it here. He loved the weather, which came in two choices: hot or hotter. He loved the back-off, laid-back, live-and-let-live attitude.

After his long stint back east on assignments, including even longer stints across the world in uncomfortable time zones and climates, he thought he just might never leave Southern California again.

He rode the elevator up, unlocked the double glass doors that led into his business and stepped inside to utter and complete quiet.

His favorite state of being, utter and complete quiet. Given that it was ten minutes to eight, that left him ten precious minutes to enjoy the solitude before his office manager and temp showed up. He hoped the temp worker was Marge, his favorite of Eddie's employees. She did her job without flapping her mouth, she was knowledgeable when it came to accounting, and because she was old enough to be his mother, he didn't have to worry about Eddie's motives for sending her. She had five kids and two grandchildren and never showed him her family pictures. He loved that about her, and he always asked for her. Eddie usually complied.

Unless he was in a mood to prove to his son that he needed some excitement. Then he'd send a cute young blonde with far more physical assets than mental capabilities. Maybe even a redhead or a brunette, but Reilly always knew when Eddie was messing with him because the temp would bat her eyes and giggle a lot and not know the difference between a debit and a credit, much less what a general ledger was.

If Eddie pulled that today, he'd just send her away. He was headed down the brick hallway toward his private office when the elevator doors dinged and opened.

Expecting Marge, he turned, but the greeting died on his tongue when one Tessa Delacantro stepped through the double glass doors.

7

TESSA'S STOMACH LODGED firmly in her throat, she stepped into the office she'd been assigned to for the next four days. The place was quiet and understated, with wood and glass accents and gorgeous views of the San Gabriel Mountains through the north windows, but that wasn't what made her freeze.

It was the man standing there staring at her as if she were a ghost.

It was the last person on earth she'd expected and the one most on her mind.

Reilly Ledger, looking pretty much exactly as she remembered him—long, lean and attitude-ridden.

He wasn't half-naked today. He wore black trousers, a black, soft-looking shirt and, big surprise, black athletic shoes. Black from head to toe. His short midnight hair still stood straight up and his eyes still reminded her of glittering blue diamonds. Trouble personified. She had no idea why he was here at her job, but a little part of her sparked to life. Had he somehow come for her? "What are you doing here?"

"I was about to ask you the same thing." His voice

was not necessarily soft or kind, but rough and serrated, and absolutely demanded an answer.

He *hadn't* come for her. Of course he hadn't. Clearly, he'd hoped to never see her again.

As for what *she* had hoped...she had no idea.

Eddie had been surprised she'd wanted to work today, but she'd needed to. There was no reason to sit in her apartment and feel sorry for herself. Sure, she'd had a bit of a trauma, but she wasn't a wilting flower. She could dive right back into her life.

Needed to dive right back.

Eddie had promised her in his gentle, warm, reassuring voice that this job would be good for her, it would be a challenge, yes, but the boss was someone special, who would take good care of her.

She certainly didn't need taking care of, but she could appreciate a soft-spoken boss, a kind soul, someone who'd just let her be and do what she did best— work with numbers. "I'm here to work," she said.

He stared at her bleakly. "You're the temp."

"Yes. I'm supposed to be at an accounting business for the next four days—" Oh God. She looked into his taut, unhappy face. "Yours," she whispered. "I'm supposed to temp...for you? I never imagined he'd—"

"Neither did I." He shook his head. "And I ate his gift of breakfast this morning. I should have known the no-good, meddling bastard was up to something when he brought me McDonald's. He's such a health nut. It was a damn bribe."

She didn't have to wonder at his edgy, unpredictable mood. As a rule, she was open to herself and all experiences and to other people being who they were. But in this case, he'd been manipulated, and a man like Reilly would hate that. Because of what happened the other night, she felt overwhelmingly conscious of him. He wasn't bulky and he certainly didn't come close enough to invade her space, but she felt an almost over-the-top awareness of him anyway. As if her every nerve ending had been exposed by just looking at him. A product of what she'd let him do to her. Begged him to do to her.

She knew why *she* was uncomfortable looking at him. He brought it all back—her neurotic behavior, the way she'd flung herself at him, everything. Oh, yes, she knew why her face was heating up even as she stood there.

But she didn't understand what was bothering *him.* He had nothing to be ashamed of; he hadn't thrown himself at her. And if it was about the work, she was a fine worker, a hard worker and a good person to boot, damn it. "I don't understand, Reilly, why you're so upset."

He just stared at her with those light eyes that so easily hid his every thought.

"I mean, yes, Eddie was a little sneaky about sending me here without telling us, but you did request a temp, right?" She purposely looked through him instead of at him because looking at him directly was like looking straight into the sun. Beautiful and dangerous all in one. "Or is it because it's...me?"

"It's nothing personal," he said. "I just work best with...a grumpy, old temp." He propped his shoulder up against the door frame and folded his arms as he eyed her. "You're not old and I doubt you have a grumpy bone in your entire body."

Wait— Was there a compliment in there somewhere?

"Where's Marge?" he asked. "I like Marge."

"Marge is maybe fifty-five and one of the nicest people I know. Hardly old and grumpy."

"She is when she's here. She smells like mothballs and snaps my head off when I talk to her."

"Maybe you bring out the worst in people," Tessa suggested, feeling a little grumpy herself now. She moved toward the reception desk and dropped her purse next to the computer, phone and adding machine. She could see down the hall where there were four doors, all closed. Glass and brick dominated the office. Not a plant or a splash of color in the place that was cool and a bit reserved.

Apparently not unlike the man she was going to work for. She forced a smile. "In any case, it looks like you're stuck with me. Where do I start?"

He just let out a long breath, his big body looking quite tense. Which actually made her mad. *She* made *him* tense? Ha! "Look, if it helps, I can be grumpy all day," she offered. "Oh, and by the way, it's really nice to see you again."

That got him. He swore softly as he shoved his fingers through his short spiky hair, making it stick up all the more.

She had no idea how in the world she ever imagined this man had a secret beta side, but one thing she knew was that she'd let him see far too much of her when they'd been at Eddie's house. Furthermore, she regretted finding him sexy, even for one little moment. She'd let him in, she'd shared some of herself and she regretted that, a lot. She'd…she'd let him kiss and touch her and she didn't even really know him.

She didn't usually do that sort of thing and knowing it had been the fright, the trauma, didn't help. She just wanted to forget the whole thing and there was only one way to do that. Without pondering it further, she grabbed her purse. "Look, I don't know why Eddie sent me over here without telling you, or me for that matter, but clearly, he made a mistake." She went back through the glass doors toward the elevator, grateful that when she punched the down button, the doors opened immediately.

She stepped inside and hit the close button, which it did, also in a timely fashion. She waited until she heard the doors touch before she turned around to face them. Slowly she let out a breath, which halted in her throat when the elevator stopped on the fourth floor.

No matter what the little hitch in her heart told her, it

wasn't Reilly coming after her. Not even a superhero could have run down a flight of stairs that fast and besides, he wasn't coming after her, he wanted her long gone.

A couple got on the elevator and it began to move again, far sooner than her heart rate returned to normal. Telling herself that she was fine, that she'd made the right decision, she pulled out her cell phone and dialed Eddie's office. She'd need a different job, pronto.

"Jeannie," she said when Eddie's secretary answered the phone. "Can you tell Eddie I need another assignment? This one didn't work out after all."

"Oh, dear," Jeannie said. "Hold please."

The elevator opened onto the lobby floor. The couple got off first, arm in arm, lost in each other's eyes. *Love you*, the man mouthed to the woman as he drew her close and the woman let out a dreamy smile in response.

Something deep within Tessa tightened at the sight. What a lovely man, so incredibly over the moon for his lover. It touched her, watching him allow his every feeling to show.

That would be something, she thought with a little sigh, having a man let his every emotion show.

"Tessa." Jeannie's voice was replaced by Eddie's in her ear. "What's the matter with my idiot son?"

"Um…" This wasn't a subject she wanted to touch with a ten-foot pole. "Well—"

"Because I already assigned everything else. There is no other job at the moment."

"You don't have anything else for me at all?" Her heart fell. She needed to work. "Are you sure?" She stepped off the elevator and ran smack into a solid brick wall of a body.

Reilly.

Mouth tight, his jaw bunching all sexylike— No, not sexy, she told herself. He was not sexy.

He gripped her shoulders in a firm grip. "Tessa."

Had she said she wanted a man to show his every emotion for her? Because here was a man doing just that, unfortunately the emotions he felt toward her were quite different than the ones she'd envisioned.

"Tessa?" Eddie said in her ear through the cell phone. "You still there?"

"Yes." She stared at Reilly. "Just call me when you have work." She shoved the phone in her purse, deciding to deal with one worry at a time. "How did you get down here so fast?"

"Stairs."

She eyed him. He would have had to haul ass down those five flights of stairs and yet he wasn't so much as breathing heavily. "You know, you really don't seem like an accountant to me."

"That's what I am."

She eyed his black clothes, his intense eyes, his incredible stillness, which alluded to an edgy but undoubtedly dangerous air. She'd kissed this man, she'd touched this man and looking at him this morning horrified her because she still didn't know who he was. "You look like you could be a bad guy."

"We've already established I'm not."

"Not a bad guy, then. A...Bond. That's it, you look like a secret agent or something. It would explain the gun you carry."

"You've got an overactive imagination."

"Let me go, Reilly."

He sighed, a sound that managed to perfectly convey his wistful thinking. "I can't."

"Of course you can, you just...let go."

"Yes, but Eddie doesn't seem to have anything else for you."

"So?"

"So I won't be the one responsible for you being out of work. Back upstairs." Then he motivated her to step back onto the elevator by taking a single step toward her.

When he followed her in, he hit the fifth-floor button and crossed his arms, staring at the closed door, completely ignoring the fact she was staring at him.

When the doors opened on the fifth floor at his offices, he looked at her.

She looked right back.

"Let's go," he said.

"I don't think so."

He pinched the bridge of his nose as if she was giving him a headache.

Because as he deserved it, she had no sympathy whatsoever.

"Why not?" he asked.

"Because you don't want me to work for you."

"I do so."

She laughed.

"Okay," he said. "So I didn't at first."

"Really." She crossed her arms, too. "What changed your mind?"

"Look, I'm a little off in the mornings."

"You're kidding."

He inhaled deeply as if he needed a cleansing breath, then grabbed her arm again and propelled her off the elevator. He opened the double glass doors for her. Once again they stood in front of the large wooden reception desk.

"Why don't we start with this?" She tossed her purse down. "Tell me what your problem is."

"I'm not sure. Seeing you threw me off." Closing the distance between them, he reached out and wrapped his fingers around the pom-pom dangling off the zipper of her sweater, which she'd zipped up to her neck against the morning chill.

He tugged.

"Hey!" She reached up, but it was too late, he'd unzipped her soft, cream-colored sweater all the way down and peeled it open. He stared down at the pale-peach shell she wore beneath. Not at the blouse, but at her exposed neck and throat, which was even more colorful today than it had been Saturday. Dark blue and purple mottled her skin.

Lightly, with a gentle touch, he settled his hand over her throat, his fingers wide. The slightly rough tips glided over her skin. In perfect contrast to the tender touch, his eyes were hot and hard with fury. "Did you see a doctor?"

"I'm okay."

"Tess—"

For some reason, the way he touched her as if she were a fragile piece of china made her eyes burn when she didn't want to feel anything for this man, especially not this crazy, inexplicable relief at being with the one person who understood what hell the weekend had held. She stepped back. "Don't. Don't you dare go all sweet on me now."

He pushed the sweater off her shoulders and down her arms. When it had fallen to the floor, he lifted her wrist and looked at the bruising there as well.

From her purse on the reception desk, her cell phone rang. With her free hand she reached for it and looked at the display. "It's Eddie."

Reilly grabbed it from her and clicked it on. "What do you want now?" He frowned as he listened. "Just relax, I'm giving her the job. But after this week, I'm switching to another temp agency. Someone who doesn't interfere with his clients' lives." He turned off the phone and tossed it back into her bag, then brought her other wrist up.

"Don't answer my phone again," she said, trying to sound strong when his touch made her weak. "It's rude."

"Yes, ma'am," he said meekly, playing at being a beta guy for a second. As if there was anything beta about him. His thumb swiped lightly over her skin. "Can you move it without pain?"

"It's not broken."

"That's not what I asked you."

"Reilly—" With him touching her, her thoughts had scattered. She couldn't even muster up a good outrage. She liked his hands on her.

Just as she had before.

Her legs felt a little shaky and her stomach quivered. It startled her to realize she didn't really have any control over her body's response to him. "I really think I should go."

"Are you good at bookkeeping?"

"I'm great at bookkeeping, but—"

"Then stay."

"I—"

"Stay," he repeated. He picked up her sweater and hung it on the standing coatrack by the doors. "Come on."

"Where to?"

He let out a breath that was nearly, but not quite, a laugh. "Not to a servant's room with nothing but a cot and not through an attic access-way either. Don't worry, Tess, today will be a cakewalk compared to what we've already done together.''

What they'd already done together.

That hung in the air for a moment and, given the way he looked at her from those depthless eyes, he was thinking about it, too.

Then he turned away to show her around. She put those memories out of her mind, thinking she had four long days here to work and it would be nothing but that. Work.

Absolutely, nothing more.

8

REILLY HAD A STAFF ROOM and three offices: one for his
office manager, one for the temps he hired and the farthest one for himself. He let Tessa into the temp's office
and tried to ignore the little voice in his head, the one
that was berating him for caving in and keeping her
there.

Tessa sat at the desk and looked at the computer,
which he leaned over her to boot up. Just as he did, his
office manager poked her head into the office, having
clearly just arrived because she held a steaming Star-
bucks coffee cup and still wore her sweater.

"You're late," he said, watching the computer screen
and not noticing that Tessa's hair smelled like something he wanted to bury his nose in.

Much.

How was it the little pixie of a woman with her long
hair and mossy eyes that flashed her every thought
could make him yearn so damn much he ached?

He hated to ache.

"If I'm late," Cheri said, casually sipping from her
cup. "It's your own fault."

"That's right," Reilly agreed. "Because everything is my fault."

"Eddie called." Cheri gave him a long, undecipherable look. "Said to make sure you don't take out your mood on anyone. Anyone being your temp today." She smiled at Tessa. "Hello, there. Has he taken his mood out on you?"

"No," Reilly said. Damn, he was going to have to introduce them. "Tessa, this is Cheri. She's my office manager—"

"Ha."

Reilly sighed. "What, now you're *not* my office manager?"

Cheri just looked at him.

"She also thinks she runs my life," he added in an aside to Tessa.

"Well, if you ran it better, then I wouldn't have to interfere," said Cheri, calmly sipping her coffee.

"In any case," he felt compelled to admit to Tessa, "she does happen to know her stuff and she'll be showing you what to do around here."

"And?" Cheri asked sweetly.

"And...lunch is at twelve?"

"And...?"

He stared at her. No, he wasn't going to do this, he wasn't going to tell Tessa—

"What he's trying to get to," Cheri said. "Is the fact that I'm also his mother. He often forgets to mention that."

Reilly closed his eyes. Opened them.

And found Tessa studying him with unabashed curiosity. "I don't know why," she said to Cheri, "but I didn't imagine he had a mother."

"I know," said his mother, smiling serenely. "He's quite annoying and stubborn, isn't he? I have to say, he didn't get either of those traits from me."

"I'm just misunderstood," Reilly said and Cheri laughed and hugged him.

Tessa remained mute but it wasn't, he was sure, out of loyalty to him. Not after how he'd treated her this morning, but honest to God, all he wanted was to just move on from what had happened Friday night.

He couldn't, however, not with her needing this job because of money. Four long days.

He was really getting tired of his father with his interfering ways, this belief that life was all about fun and laughter—often at his own son's expense.

Tessa was still watching him with those eyes. And then there were the bruises on her delicate throat. They were killing him.

So, fine. She was going to be in his hair for a few days. At least she smelled good.

If only he didn't remember that she tasted even better.

SOMEHOW REILLY MANAGED to put Tess out of his head and bury himself in work. Thankfully he'd picked an occupation he was well-suited to and was good at.

Numbers didn't argue, numbers didn't manipulate. Numbers just let him be.

Overall, he supposed, things went well. They all stayed busy and Tessa actually did know her way around an accounting ledger.

At the end of the day, she appeared in the doorway of his office, her eyes shining, her mouth curved in a smile as she held out a stack of files he'd asked Cheri for.

He couldn't help but notice that she had been enjoying herself since he'd convinced her to stay. But he had a feeling she always enjoyed herself, enjoyed life. Damned if that wasn't unexpectedly attractive.

"I brought the Sarkins files up to date, all the way through to the general ledger," she said. "And Cheri and I together handled the Anderson account as well." She started to go, then stopped. "Oh, and your father's on line two."

He picked up the phone. "After what you've pulled," he said to Eddie. "I am not going out with you and a pack of women to the game tonight."

Eddie's long-suffering sigh sounded in his ear. "I told you, no pack of women. Just a couple. And that's not why I called."

"You want me to thank you for the old, grumpy office help?"

"That's no way to talk about your own mother."

"You know damn well I'm referring to Tessa."

"Who's not old and grumpy."

Reilly drew in a deep breath and looked at Tess, who was still standing there. "Which is my point."

"She's good, isn't she?"

"You know she is. Look, I don't know what you're up to, but—"

"Son, I'd love to stick around and listen to you sound like an ass, but I have a bigger problem than even you at the moment."

"What are you talking about?"

"The burglary…you remember the four guys the police hauled in?"

Yes, he was fairly certain he remembered.

"Well, apparently a few of them have prior records and when the cops held those up, dangling some sort of deal, they squealed like the three little pigs. They said the whole thing was set up by someone I knew. It turns out she's…"

Reilly waited impatiently. "*She's* what?"

Eddie sighed and said, "An ex of mine."

"An ex. Shocking. Do they have any idea which one of the thousands it might be?"

"There weren't thousands. Hundreds maybe, but—"

"Get to the point, Eddie."

"It was Sheila Vanetti. Your mother always refers to her as the crazy one and it turns out, she's right."

"Where is she now?"

"Missing, funny enough, and the police haven't been able to track her down. And they think…well, this is embarrassing, to tell you the truth."

"They think what?"

"That she's trying to scare me," Eddie said laughing. "Funny, right?"

"Oh, yeah," Reilly said. "A laugh riot."

"They even think I need protection. Can you imagine such a thing? Me being stalked? How hysterical is that?"

"Hysterical." *Christ.* "Did you hire a bodyguard?"

His mother appeared in the doorway. She'd always had a sort of sixth sense when it came to Eddie and, sure enough, she wore her worried frown.

"I thought," Eddie said, "that given your last occupation, you could handle it for me."

"I'll be right over."

"Thanks, son."

When he'd hung up, Tessa said, "Is everything okay?"

He rubbed his eyes. "Not really."

"What is it, Reilly?" This from Cheri, who looked far more worried than an ex should look. But he told them everything and, when he was finished, both of them watched him with that look that said they believed he could do anything.

Apparently Eddie thought so as well.

All these damn tugs at his heart. And he didn't have a clue what to do about them.

9

THE NEXT MORNING, Tessa turned the key of her VW Beetle, but for the second morning in a row, nothing happened. Yesterday she'd thought it was just a dead battery and she'd charged it overnight.

Apparently she'd been wrong. "Come on, baby," she coaxed, and tapped the console lovingly. She tried again.

Nothing.

With a sigh, she leaned back. Her sister had already left for work, so she couldn't get a ride from her. If she called Rafe, he'd probably get on the next plane.

She couldn't call Eddie again.

So she got on the bus and decided not to worry about her car until she could do something about it. By the time she got onto the elevator in Reilly's building, it was one minute after eight and her heart was pumping. She hated to be late and she ran off the elevator the moment the doors opened.

"I'm sorry," she said breathlessly to Cheri, who stood there stripping off her sweater, clearly having also just arrived.

"No need to be sorry, you're close enough." Cheri

smiled. "And since you're holding a Krispy Kreme doughnut bag in your hand, you're my new best friend."

Tessa laughed. "It's a shameless bribe for your son, but I brought enough for all of us. I'm determined to see him smile today."

"Now that I'd like to see. He's working out now; there's a gym on the fourth floor he sometimes uses in the mornings. Between that and the doughnuts, it might just do the trick." Cheri turned on the stereo to soft rock, opened the shades to the beautiful view and flipped on the lights to the hall that led to the offices.

Apparently there wasn't a regular receptionist, because there wasn't enough phone traffic to warrant one, which left the two of them taking turns answering phones. Knowing Reilly liked his messages first-thing, Tessa sat at the front desk to check his machine.

"He's not easy to get to know," Cheri said behind her. "And yet you already seem to have him pegged."

"Yes, well, we got what you might call concentrated time together that night we spent locked up in Eddie's house," Tessa reminded her.

"It's funny what the long nighttime hours will do to a person when they're awake," Cheri said. "How much more open you can be, how much more you'll share."

Tessa had to smile wryly at that. They might not have shared a lot of words, per se, but there'd been enough kissing and touching to make her feel extremely open. And vulnerable.

She wasn't comfortable with that. Not one little bit.

"Is that what happened, Tessa?"

She sighed. "In a manner of speaking. And now, in the light of day, facing each other over accounting ledgers, it's been a little...awkward. Sometimes a lot awkward."

"Plus, Reilly has a way of making things as awkward as possible, doesn't he?" Cheri said, smiling sympathetically. "I love him, I love him with my entire heart and soul and yet I want to just smack him sometimes for not letting people...I don't know...*see* him. He's so afraid he's going to end up like his father. He's a bit hung up on his privacy."

"I noticed."

"He doesn't get that from me, I'll tell you that. Actually, I don't know where he gets it. Probably from working for the government as an operative doing...well, I'm not really sure, to tell you the truth. I'm just glad he's not still doing it."

Tessa stopped in the act of opening the bag of doughnuts. "You mean he was...CIA?"

"Was." Cheri winced. "He didn't tell you."

"No. But it explains a lot. Why did he get out of it?"

Cheri took a moment to answer. "Let's just say his last mission nearly killed him. Literally. It made him wary. And unhappy, I think. In any case, it took him a long time to recover and in some ways he's still recovering." She put her hand on Tessa's wrist. "You'll be patient with him, won't you Tessa? Patient, and kind, and compassionate?"

"I'm sorry for what he went through, but I think you have the wrong idea—"

"You like him," Cheri said. "You care about him. I can see that."

"I barely know him." And because she didn't want to talk about it anymore, she busied herself with sharpening a pencil.

Cheri took the hint and left her alone. Tessa stared at the electric pencil sharpener, her mind far from the pencil and stuck on Reilly.

He'd been in the CIA. He'd been hurt.

He'd become wary because of it.

He needed patience. Kindness and compassion.

She had those things, but she wasn't sure Cheri knew what she was asking. Reilly didn't want anything from her but work.

A few moments later, Cheri handed her a stack of work and gave her a little smile. "Are you going to offer me a doughnut or are you just going to torture me with the scent of them all morning?"

Tessa set them out. She took the stack of work and a glazed doughnut and went to her desk to dig in. After a while, Cheri popped her head into the room and said she was going out to run some errands.

Alone, Tessa went into the small photocopy-fax room and started making a stack of copies she needed for one of Reilly's clients. She got into a rhythm of lifting the top of the machine, replacing the sheet she needed copied, placing it back into the file. The sound of the copier was loud and hypnotic, so that when someone stepped up right behind her suddenly, she let out a little scream and jerked. Papers went flying as she whirled around, flattening herself back against the machine.

"Hey. Hey, it's just me." Reilly. He stood there, all in black, of course. Black athletic shoes, black running shorts, black T-shirt, which was plastered to him. The man sure was in some kind of amazing shape. She registered this in a distant way because he'd nearly given her heart failure and she couldn't talk. He definitely looked the secret agent part, she'd give him that. Tall, edgy, dangerous....

"Tess?"

Get it together, she told herself, *get it together before you annoy the hell out of him for acting like a baby.* "I'm sorry. I'm fine." She bent for the papers.

"Are you sure?" He hunkered down beside her and started helping her.

"No, I've got it." She shoved the stack all back into the file, figuring she'd fix it when she was alone and could breathe again. "I'm just fine. Really."

"All right." He eyed her carefully. "I'm going to shower in the bathroom in my office." He paused. "I didn't mean to scare you."

"I just thought I was alone, that's all. Cheri said you

were working out." He looked good all hot and sweaty and bothered. Extremely superhero-like.

Had she ever really seen a different side of him, a soft and gentle side, even for a moment? No. She had to have imagined that, because this man with his see-through eyes and rock-hard body and low, rough voice didn't have a soft and gentle side—

He reached out, dispersing her thoughts like the wind. His hand settled on her shoulder and squeezed it lightly. "It's okay, you know, it's just delayed shock." Standing, he pulled her up. "I...know what you're going through."

Oh, damn. He knew. He knew because something terrible had happened to him on his last mission, something much more terrible than being held up in Eddie's house. He was big and tough and strong, and yet he understood, and wanted her to know that.

He needs kindness and compassion and patience, Cheri had told her and yet here he was offering it to her. She stared down at the papers, which suddenly went a little blurry, because here was that flash of beta guy again and it confused her.

With a sigh, he took the stack and set it all on the copier. He put his hands on her again, her hips this time.

"I'm really fine," she whispered, wanting it to be so. Wanting it to be so quite badly.

"Yes."

She shifted a little closer, needing the contact, needing...so much.

"Don't." His voice was low, gruff, and he tried to hold her off. "I'm all sweaty."

"I don't care."

"Tess." But he pulled her just a little closer, waiting until she tipped her head up to his.

"You know what?" she whispered. "I think I lied. I don't think I'm so fine. It..." She closed her eyes and saw the gray room. Saw Reilly standing in Eddie's kitchen with a gun. "It keeps coming back."

"I'm sorry." He looked her over, his jaw going all tight and bunched and sexy when he took in the bruises on her throat. "I'm really sorry."

Something deep within her curled, warmed. *Ached.* "Maybe you should go back to snarling at me."

"I don't snarl at you," he said, grimacing. "I never mean to, anyway. Not at you."

Oh, no. He was making her melt again, melt into a boneless heap. The way he looked at her, as if she was something he needed to run from and run to at the same time... Without permission, her arms snaked upward around his neck and held on for dear life so that he couldn't change his mind and back away. Her chest brushed his. So did her thighs. And everything in between.

Every single erogenous zone in her body stood up and took notice.

His fingers tightened on her hips for one moment, then he dropped his hands from her and stood back.

Which was a good thing. It reminded her why she was here. Work. Just work.

She didn't want to feel this tug for him. She wanted him to go far, far away and leave her to that work be-

fore she forgot her entire humiliating experience with
him at Eddie's and did something stupid.

Like kiss him for a third time.

Oh, no. No, the next time they kissed, *he* was going to
initiate it. *He* was going to want it. Because she already
knew that if he did kiss her, she'd give in, she'd let him
do it. She'd let him kiss them both senseless.

And then he'd walk away. Pretend it didn't happen.
She didn't have to be ex-CIA to know that.

But he didn't kiss her.

Not even once.

THE NEXT DAY Reilly was on his way into the office
when Cheri called him on his cell phone.

"Oh, honey. Glad I caught you. I'm not working for
you today."

Reilly had already gone for his run that morning and
was eating his way through a fast-food breakfast as he
drove. He knew the two cancelled each other out, but
he didn't care. He ran because it felt good and he ate
what he ate because it tasted good. "Are you sick?" he
asked her.

"I'm never sick."

Oka-a-ay. "Attitude adjustment day?"

"Why would I need that, I don't have an attitude."

"So it's...a woman thing?" he asked warily, not really wanting to know.

"Reilly, I'm working for your father today. He's behind, and—"

"*What?*"

"And I've got you all caught up, so—"

"But..." This was so far from what he expected, he couldn't think. "You work for me."

"Yes," Cheri said with that calm reasonableness she had, that made his brain feel like she was scrambling it. "But he needs me."

"But..."

"Reilly, honey, honestly. Tessa could do my job blindfolded. You'll be fine."

He nearly missed his turnoff. "But Tessa isn't my office manager. You are."

"And I need a day off."

"To work for Eddie."

"That's right."

This made no sense. "You want to work for the man who deserted you when you were a pregnant teenager."

"Oh, for God's sake," Cheri said, making an annoyed sound. "Look, it's time you knew this. *I'm* the one who jumped his bones when I was sixteen. And I'm the one who—"

"*Jeez!*" He nearly rear-ended the car in front of him. "*Over-share!*"

"I knew the chance I was taking," she said calmly. "We've long ago established how naive I was, but if you think I have regrets you're the naive one."

"Mom." She was certifiable. "He has a hundred other women he could use for today."

"Yes, but he wants me. And let's face it, I'm the best."

"What about whoever he took to Cabo?"

"Well, I doubt whoever she was knew accounting."

True.

"Stop acting like an old man, Reilly. I'll be back in a few days. Live a little while I'm gone, okay?"

"You sound just like him when you say that," he said, broodingly.

"Have a good day, honey."

He stared down at his cell after she hung up on him, then tossed it onto the passenger seat. *Live a little.* He'd lived plenty. He'd lived long and hard, and frankly, was happy with how things were going. Nice and quiet and even-keeled. No surprises. No being konked over the head by idiotic burglars. No being kissed stupid by a little hottie who had somehow—and he was still dizzy over this one—ended up working for him.

By the time he got into his office, he was ready to bury himself in numbers. Lots of numbers.

Tessa sat behind the front desk on the phone, her brown hair swinging as she turned to watch him walk in. Her big, bright-green eyes gave away her every thought, as usual.

She was thinking she would have been happier if he hadn't shown up.

Join the club, baby.

She recovered nicely, even gave him a little wave accompanied by what seemed like a very genuine smile. So genuine he nearly waved right back.

"I'll be sure to note the changes to the payables," she said sweetly into the phone. "Oh, why, yes, I'll tell Mr. Ledger that you think I'm the very best temp he's ever had," she said, laughing. "Just so happens that I think so, too. Bye, now." She hung up and sent him a saucy look that dared him to say otherwise.

"Maybe you should tell Eddie you need a raise," he suggested.

"Then he'll charge you more."

"I can handle Eddie."

She smiled. "So can I."

"I don't imagine there isn't much you can't handle," he heard himself say.

"Nope. That comes from being the baby of the family," she said proudly. "My sister and brother like to worry about me, but it's their own fault I'm this way. They created me."

"So you're close to them."

"Very."

"They probably don't try to run your life," he muttered, thinking of his mother.

She laughed at that. "Are you kidding? They live to run my life. That's what love's all about, Reilly."

Yeah. Love. He forced his eyes off her and the sunshine-yellow suit dress she wore and looked around the counter that just yesterday had held a bag of Krispy Kreme doughnuts.

"Oh, I'm sorry," she said, reading his mind. "I'm fresh out of cash until payday."

Ah, hell. He came back toward her. "Don't buy me doughnuts with your own money. There's no need. There's petty cash in Cheri's desk."

"But then it'd be *you* buying you doughnuts."

"Yes, and then no one owes anyone anything."

She just looked at him.

Resisting the urge to squirm, he walked past her and headed down the hall toward his office.

"Good thing Cheri told me you weren't a morning person," she muttered.

Which stopped him in his tracks.

"She also said you're not an afternoon or evening person," she said. "In case you were wondering."

He had to ask, even knowing he shouldn't. "What else did she say about me?"

Her smile widened just a little bit wickedly.

He did squirm now.

"She said you're egotistical, grumpy, stubborn and innately suspicious."

Okay, that he could handle, as it was true.

But then she put a finger to her chin as she thought. "Oh, and that she felt none of those things were your fault."

"Really? Why not?"

"Because she and your father screwed you up and what they didn't screw up, working for the CIA finished off."

10

"CHERI TOLD YOU all that," Reilly said slowly.

"Yep." Tess nodded. "But I already knew you weren't just some ordinary accountant. You had big, tough, alpha male written all over you the moment I first laid eyes on you. Even half-naked and holding your bruised head, I knew."

He really should have stopped for caffeine. In his present state, he wasn't equipped to deal with this. He rubbed his temples. "What else?"

"She said you need kindness and compassion."

Because, apparently, he was pretty damn pathetic. "You know, for future reference, when someone asks you a question like 'what else did they say?' and when that something else is so blatantly negative, you should probably just keep it to yourself."

She cocked her head and said, "I didn't realize you weren't looking for the truth. You seem like a guy who appreciates the truth."

He moved toward her yet again, because apparently he hadn't tortured himself enough when it came to her. "I know I'm going to regret asking this, but why were you two talking about me in the first place?"

"Cheri said I should forgive you for being such a jerky boss, that you didn't mean to be so short and abrupt all the time."

"And she said this because...?"

"Because you'd just reminded me that you needed the Morrow file, when you'd already told me three times, and I was still on the phone with another client. You didn't appear very happy with me, even though I was doing my best."

He stared at her. Had he done that? Obviously he had, but coming out of her mouth he sure sounded like an ass....

"She also said that despite your impatience, your rudeness and your temper, you have a heart of gold and, if I stayed long enough, I'd see it for myself. She told me not to let you scare me off."

Suddenly, he was glad his mother wasn't there because he had the urge to wrap his hands around her meddling neck.

"And then I said that not much could scare me off—" She broke off and looked away for a moment, as both of them clearly remembered what exactly *did* scare her.

Armed burglars.

"And then I told her," she whispered, "that I already knew you had a heart of gold and I wasn't going anywhere until the job was done, which it will be in two more days."

He stopped fantasizing about strangling Cheri and

took a closer look at the woman in front of him. She was small, almost deceptively fragile and yet, he knew damn well how much inner strength she had. More than any woman he'd ever met. "I don't have a heart of gold. Not even close."

"We met under unusual circumstances," she said, still very quietly. "It accelerated everything. Don't say that isn't true."

"Tess—"

"You saved me that night."

"Anyone would have done the same."

"No."

He let out a disparaging breath, and she got up out of her chair and came around the desk to stand right in front of him. "You saved me and I've never even thanked you."

"Don't." God. He couldn't take that. Without even knowing why, he reached for her hand. "And don't make me out to be someone I'm not."

"I just want to know more about you." She lifted her face. "Cheri told me something bad happened to you on your last job. That you've been messed up because of it."

"Cheri talks too much."

Her other hand came up and sandwiched his, then she brought it up between her breasts, against her heart, which he could feel beating strong and steadily.

"I promised myself I wasn't going to touch you," she

said. "But then you touched my hand and..." She smiled a little. "And I can't seem to resist."

"I shouldn't have touched you at all. Ever."

"It's too late. Did you know...?"

"What?"

"That I've been the one to kiss you, every time?"

He couldn't take his eyes off her mouth. "Have you?"

"Yes. And next time...if there is a next time, you'll have to kiss me."

He absolutely was *not* going to do that. Her lips were naked and parted, and now he had to close his eyes. Probably. He *probably* wasn't going to kiss her.

"Tell me what makes you so...stoic," she said softly.

"Just because I don't talk every moment of the day doesn't mean I'm stoic."

She let out a little laugh and said, "Okay, maybe stoic isn't the right word. But distant isn't either, or cold." She tilted her head and dropped her gaze to his lips, which reminded him of how they felt on hers.

"Definitely not distant," she whispered. "Or cold."

He groaned; he couldn't help it. His hands dropped down to her hips and dragged her closer. "You drive me crazy."

"Why?"

"You make me want." He dropped his forehead to hers. "I don't want to want, damn it."

"Because of what happened to you?" She cupped his face. "Oh, Reilly. Did you get your heart broken?"

Broken, tromped on and destroyed, but that was another story. "She shouldn't have told you I was in the
CIA. She shouldn't have told you that my last job went
bad, that I was betrayed by a double agent who just
happened to be sleeping with me at the time."

Her eyes softened even more and she slid her arms
around his neck. "She didn't tell me that part, she
never said... How badly were you hurt?"

"I don't want—"

"Please, Reilly. Please tell me."

It was the last thing he wanted to do, but he had to
tell her something so it might as well be the truth.
"Look, I was stuffed in a trunk for a few days and left
to die," he said, shrugging. "I'm over it."

Now those eyes went suspiciously bright. Wet, shiny
moss. "My God," she whispered on a wavering breath
as she hugged him so tightly he could barely breathe.
"No wonder."

"No wonder what?"

"No wonder you don't like people close. You were
hurt by someone you let in."

"Not that hurt."

"And no wonder you're an accountant. You get to
work alone. With numbers instead of people, for the
most part."

He didn't know what to do with the fact she saw him
so clearly. "I was an accountant for the CIA, too, before
the field stuff. I was an analyst."

"Everything makes so much sense now. Like why you're afraid of the dark."

He wasn't afraid of the dark.

He wasn't afraid of anything.

She skimmed her mouth over his jaw, leaving soft, short sweet little kisses as she worked her way over his flesh.

In reaction, his stomach tightened. Other parts did, too.

And as it turned out, he *was* afraid of something.

He was afraid of her. "Tess, I thought you weren't going to kiss me—"

"I haven't, not really. It doesn't count unless I touch your lips with mine, which if you'll notice, I didn't do."

He'd noticed. It was just that his body didn't seem to be able to comprehend the difference, not one little bit. "Tess—"

"I like the way you shorten my name," she whispered, and wrapped her arms around his shoulders. "I like that a lot. Reilly—"

Whatever it was, he didn't want to hear it right now. He was a fraction of an inch from caving in, from giving in to her warm, giving body. He was so close to kissing her, all because she had eyes that sucked him in and a voice that he'd follow anywhere.

Because he had to, he set her away from him, this woman who seemed to personify temptation. "We have work," he said. "Lots and lots of work."

"Right."

Her eyes told him that he could put this off for however long he wanted, but it wasn't over.

And he found he was afraid of one more thing.

He was afraid she was right.

11

TESSA WORKED HARD for the rest of the day. She had no problems without Cheri, just double the work. That was okay with her, she loved being busy, loved being needed.

In her life there weren't a lot of people who depended on her or needed her for anything. She and her friends were more casual than close. Then there were her siblings, who'd always taken on the authority role, or at least they thought they had. They'd laugh if Tessa tried to get them to need her in any way. As frustrating as it sometimes was, she felt quite certain they still thought of her as a little, snotty-nosed kid.

Not as a woman.

But she was. She was a woman who loved responsibility and tethers on her heart. She craved them.

And yet she couldn't seem to get them.

But this job...it was good. It made her feel important. She sat surrounded by numbers and ledgers and accounts, thoroughly engrossed, so engrossed she nearly fell out of her chair when a Taco Bell bag suddenly appeared in front of her face.

"Just me." Reilly dropped it onto the accounts receivable report she'd been lost in. "You're getting better. You didn't jump all the way out of your skin that time."

She had no idea why she liked that he noticed she still felt a little jumpy. She had no idea why watching him watch her made her feel a little...soft. Feminine. "I didn't even hear you leave."

"I know. You get pretty into your work."

"I'm single-minded," she agreed. "My family doesn't think that's a virtue."

"There's nothing wrong with single-mindedness when you're in accounting. Now, maybe if you were an air traffic controller or something..."

She laughed, though emotion backed up in her throat a little when he smiled. Good Lord, he should do that more often.

"Anyway..." he said, plowing his free hand through his hair, as if it wasn't standing straight up already. "My stomach's growling. It's lunchtime."

She glanced at the wall clock. One o'clock. No wonder she felt light-headed. "So, did you take the money from petty cash? Because the boss doesn't like it when you spend money on another employee here."

"Consider it payback for the doughnuts."

"I didn't buy you the doughnuts so you'd buy me lunch," she said, opening the bag and the heavenly scent of a steak quesadilla wafted up. "But I'm so glad you did." She took a large bite. "Where's yours?"

Looking amused, he watched her stuff her face, then

lifted another bag and a drink-holder with two large sodas in it. "I thought we'd actually eat at a table. Like in the staff room—"

"Oh." Embarrassed, she licked the cheese off her lips and laughed. "Right." She stood up and grabbed the quesadilla. She followed him down the hall and into the small room designated as the staff room. There was a refrigerator, a well-stocked little pantry she suspected Cheri took care of and a small wooden table with four chairs around it.

He pulled out a chair for her, waiting for her to sit and she suddenly felt a little off-kilter. A little nervous.

They were on a lunch date. Sort of.

"What's the matter?" he said, handing her a drink.

"It's our first date. It feels a little weird," she admitted. "Given that we've already slept together."

"Eating at work does not constitute a date. And we didn't exactly sleep together." That said, he took a large bite out of his chicken soft taco.

She tried not to name the emotion that went through her at his words, but it felt an awful lot like disappointment. "So what *would* constitute a date?"

In the act of adding hot sauce to his taco, he paused, then said, "I don't even know. I haven't actually dated in a long time. Not since…"

Not since he'd been betrayed while at the CIA. He didn't say it; he didn't have to. She hated that he'd been hurt and was shocked at the thoughts of violence that flowed through her for the woman who'd done it. "What was her name?"

"Her real one? Or her alias? I knew her as Loralee. And we didn't date in the traditional sense. We were always out of the country, on various missions. Dating was impossible."

"What about before her?"

He took a bite and chewed while he thought about that. "I hate to admit this, but I can't remember."

"That's just sad, Reilly."

"Really?" he said, smiling as he took another bite. Chewed some more. Eyed her just a little knowingly. "So, what have *you* done in the dating department lately?"

The big zip, not that she wanted to admit it, so she busied herself pulling apart her quesadilla.

"Well?"

She met his gaze and then laughed sheepishly. "Okay, so we're tied. We both are equally pathetic when it comes to the opposite sex."

"Oh, no," he said silkily and brushed off his hands. His gaze ran over her features. "I never said I was pathetic with the opposite sex."

Her tummy quivered just a little. "I think I hear your phone ringing."

He cocked his head. "Chicken, Tess? Now, after all we've done?"

"All we've done is kiss," she whispered.

"More than kissed."

"We've...touched."

"Yeah. Did it feel pathetic to you?"

"No."

"Are you sure?" His voice was low, hypnotic and so sexy her entire body hummed. "Because maybe you need me to prove to you that I'm not a bungling idiot when it comes to physical matters with the opposite sex." His eyes flamed. "That I do know what I'm doing."

Oh boy. "I—" She broke off when his cell phone rang, grateful because she had no idea what she would have said anyway.

Reilly pulled the cell phone out of his pocket and frowned at the ID. "Eddie."

"Maybe he's going to give you back Marge."

He looked at her, startled, as if the thought had left his mind and was back only because she'd reminded him. She found a laugh. "Don't tell me you've forgotten you didn't want me to work here."

"You know, you're just about the most upfront woman I've ever met."

"It's a curse. Are you going to answer the phone?"

He sighed and did just that. The irritation left his face after he said hello and listened. His mouth pulling into a frown, he stood up. "An hour ago? And you're just now telling me?"

Tessa tried to look busy gathering their trash as she shamelessly eavesdropped.

"How did they get in?" He shut his eyes and shook his head as he listened. "I'll be right there— No, I do think it's necessary."

"Is he okay?" Tessa asked as soon as he clicked off.

"Yeah. Apparently the man has nine lives."

"What happened?"

He stopped at the door. "Someone went after him in the garage but they got away when Eddie managed to set off the alarm. I'm going over there now to check on him for myself."

He was going to check on the man he didn't want to be like. The man who he felt hadn't been a good father. The man who annoyed him at every turn.

A little burst of warmth spread through her, because she just realized...Reilly Ledger could play bad-ass, tough guy all he wanted, but inside there *was* a soft spot for the people in his life, whether he liked it or not.

Now all she had to do was deal with that, deal with how she felt about him.

She had a feeling she already knew how she felt about him and it was fairly terrifying.

EDDIE HUNG UP the phone and glanced over at the woman sitting at his kitchen table.

"Well?" she asked.

"Well, he didn't ask for Marge back." He thought over the implications of the telling omission. "I consider that a good sign, don't you?"

His temp for the day smiled at him and he felt his heart tip onto its side. Her smile had always done that to him.

"Maybe he's beginning to like his current temp," Cheri said softly and rose. She came to him and held an ice pack to his split lip. "You're still bleeding."

"It's nothing." He pulled it away so he could talk better because this subject was extremely important. "How can that be, him liking Tessa? She's young and pretty and smart and outgoing," he huffed and then winced because it hurt his mouth. "She's everything he doesn't want."

"Only because *you* think she's young and pretty and smart and outgoing," Cheri pointed out reasonably and put the ice pack on his lip again.

"I don't think that about her for me. I think that about her for him," Eddie said around the ice and blinked when Cheri laughed at him.

"I know that, silly man." She cupped his cheek and his heart tipped again.

"It's just that I feel a spark between them." Eddie put his hand on her hip to keep her next to him. "And it excites me because it's the first spark I've seen in Reilly in a good, long time." He knew damn well his cool, distant son went to extremes in order to not be like him.

Well, the hell with that. If he had to help things along by teaching Reilly there was fun out there to be had, then that's what he'd do. He'd already started. He'd sent Marge out on a weeklong job in downtown Pasadena, where she was happy as could be. There were two bonuses in that. One, Eddie could stay involved in what was going on at Reilly's, which he enjoyed. And two, with Tessa working for Reilly, it meant he just might be able to finagle getting Cheri to keep working for *him*.

Two birds with one stone, and everyone was happy.

Well, at least *he* was.

"Are you sure you're okay?" Cheri asked, holding the ice pack to him with one hand and using the other to touch the bruise on his cheek. "Are you sure that you don't want to go to the doctor—"

"It was just a scuffle. The lights were off in the garage or I'd have been able to get a better hold of him." He grunted. "The asshole didn't even stick around and fight like a man. Once I popped him in the eye, he was gone."

"You were too much for him." She kissed his bruised cheek and he resisted, barely, the urge to turn his head and line up their mouths. "We have work," she reminded him gently.

"Work can wait."

"You're fretting over this."

"I'm not fretting."

"Yes, you are." She ran her hand down his arm in what was supposed to be a soothing gesture, but he didn't want her to soothe him, he wanted...so damn much more.

"You fret," she repeated. "Because you want him to like you. Then you try too hard and you end up pushing him away. Leave it, Eddie." Her hands were gentle on him, so gentle. "It'll work out."

Eddie sighed, in bliss, in frustration. "He's on his way over here. He won't come see me just to see me, but because some jerk is trying to get revenge, he'll come."

"It's not some jerk. You know who it is."

Eddie sighed again and said, "Yeah."

"Oh, Eddie." Cheri gave him a hug. "You try too hard."

"The boy is hardheaded."

"Really? And where do you think he got it?" She kissed him on the cheek when he just stared at her. "It'll be all right, Eddie. It will." Another stroke of her hand. "Look at how he's running over here to save the day. He loves you. He's always loved you."

Eddie couldn't resist another second. He pulled her in for a hug. "How the hell did I ever let you get away?" he whispered into her hair, her long, glorious, dark hair. "I was such an idiot."

"Yes," Cheri agreed, and stepped back. "We were both idiots. Now, let's work. After all, that's why you brought me here, right?"

Here's your chance, Ace. Be smooth, be debonair, do your thing. Instead, his mouth went dry and he stood there like a fool. A tongueless fool. Eddie Ledger, legendary lady-killer, known for his charm and wit and ability to get any woman he ever wanted into his bed, and he couldn't come up with a single intelligent thing to say.

She stroked his jaw and moved away, moved toward his home office.

And all he could do was watch her go.

Oh, yeah, he really was just one big, fancy idiot.

TESSA GOT UP EARLY the next morning, got ready in record time and, for the first time in the history of her existence, left for work with time to spare.

When she opened her front door, Carolyn popped her head out of her apartment next door. "Hey, there.

Wow, you're..." She glanced at her watch. "*Twenty minutes early?*" Her welcoming smile vanished. "What's the matter?"

"Nothing." Tessa locked her front door and crossed her fingers that her car would start today.

"Uh-huh. Nothing." Carolyn eyed her carefully from head to toe. "You look good. New clothes?"

So she'd splurged on the way home last night, buying a new dress for work, and only partly because it was red and made her feel sexy. "This old thing?"

Carolyn didn't buy it. She put her hand on her hip. "There's a guy at work, right?"

Oh, yeah, there was a guy. But if her sister got wind of it, there'd be no peace. "There's work at work."

"So everything's okay?"

She put her Sunday best smile on. "Of course."

"You're just...early. For no special reason."

"Yep."

Carolyn crossed her arms. "Honey, I know you, and I know something's up. So you might as well spare us both the time and tell me what's going on."

"What's going on is me loving my job."

"You're sure?"

"Absolutely sure."

Carolyn eyed her for another long moment before she was satisfied. "So, are we on for dessert and a movie tomorrow night?"

"Of course."

"Great." Carolyn kissed her on the cheek. "Have a good day, hon."

And Tessa might have, if her car had started.

She sat there in her uncooperative VW and sighed. It was temping to run back to her sister for help, but this was her life, her problem, and she wanted to handle it on her own. Always being rescued by a sibling didn't count as handling it on her own.

She took the bus again. Once inside Reilly's building, she got off on the fourth floor where she knew he sometimes worked out. Oops, funny how that had happened, her getting off on the wrong floor...

She looked through the glass doors of the gym. The room was lined with exercise equipment and filled with early worker bees, all of whom were in various stages of sweating. Serious, intent faces abounded everywhere.

Tessa stood there for a moment trying to decide if she felt any remorse at all for having such a serious aversion to exercise.

Nope. No remorse at all.

She recognized some of the people she'd run into all week—the croissant lady from the lobby, the attorney from the second floor... And there, in the far corner, facing the wall of windows that opened to the beautiful San Gabriel Mountains, running on a treadmill was her temporary boss.

Headphones on his ears, he ran for all he was worth. His T-shirt clung to him, delineating every muscle, every nuance in his long, sleek back and arms. His legs pumped, burning calories. As if he needed to! The man didn't have a single inch of excess anywhere.

Her eyes caught and held on to his very fine backside.

She took a quick moment to glance furtively around, making sure no one caught her staring at his butt.

No one even looked her way.

She liked this fourth floor, she liked it a lot. She liked to see Reilly all tall, dark and sweaty and she stood there for one long moment, just soaking him in. How many times had she told herself she wasn't going to want him? And how many times had it not mattered?

She still wanted him.

Then suddenly, Reilly turned and looked unerringly right at her. His skin gleamed, his eyes glittered and his body made her knees knock together as he slowly cocked a brow, silently asking her what the hell she was doing standing there with her eyes locked on him.

Yikes. Like the calm, steady woman she was not, she turned and fled.

THIRTY MINUTES LATER, Tessa froze when the elevator dinged its arrival. From her perch at the receptionist's desk where she sat pretending to go through the messages on Reilly's answering machine, she stared at the elevator doors, her heart galloping.

What would she say to him? She hadn't a clue, she had no excuse, nothing prepared—

The doors opened. Reilly stepped off. "Morning," he said, and without a word about her Peeping Tomina act, he strode down the hall, leaving her staring after him.

In fact, he never said a word about it or how it'd gone for him at Eddie's the day before. She assumed Eddie was safe enough for now, but she'd have liked to hear that for sure.

In fact, Reilly sat holed up in his office all day and when she came in to say goodbye, he thanked her for all she'd done.

Composed and cool as ever.

She'd actually forgotten that it was over, that he'd hired her through Thursday only and she nodded to herself as she left. It had come to an end, she'd known it would.

No big deal.

It was just a very small part of her had hoped he'd hire her on permanently, maybe even admit to needing her. Her. Not Marge, not any other temp who could have done the work, but her.

Hadn't happened, and as always when she fell, she picked herself up, dusted herself off and went on her merry way.

12

THE WEEKEND CAME and Tessa spent Saturday getting her car fixed and putting the charges on her poor credit card.

When Rafe found out what she'd spent, he couldn't understand why she hadn't called him for help.

Carolyn couldn't understand why Tessa hadn't come to her to borrow the money.

And her parents fussed and fretted over the fact she hadn't let them buy her a new car last Christmas when they'd wanted.

Sure, being smothered by family was just a part of being a Delacantro, but she did her best to remain true to herself and was happier for it. She loved her family so much, but she was living her own life, handling her own responsibilities and thriving that way.

On Sunday, she and her sister went shopping and she was quite proud of the fact that she restrained herself from buying anything but new underwear, because let's face it, she didn't need another red, hot dress that would go unnoticed.

"Hmm," was all her sister said as they stood in line

at the lingerie shop with Tessa's satin, purple panties and matching bra between them.

"Do you have something to say?" Tessa asked. "Because let me remind you, you bought black lace two weeks ago, remember? Did I say 'hmm' in that snooty tone to you then?"

"No, you smirked and wondered if Rob was going to get to see them."

"A reasonable question since you've been dating him for months."

"Dating, not sleeping with."

"And why is that again?"

Her sister sighed. "I don't know. He doesn't even make a move. It's such a waste of a good relationship."

Tessa sighed inwardly and wished for a good relationship, to waste or otherwise.

ON MONDAY MORNING, she got an early morning call from Eddie, letting her know Reilly needed a temp for another week. Was she up for it?

Was she up for it? Well, given the way her heart had taken off, pounding against her ribs at just the thought of another week at Reilly's office, yes. She was most definitely up for it.

Damn it.

She tried to take her time getting ready, tried not to care what she wore or how it looked. Most of all, she tried to be in her usual running-out-the-door-at-the-last-moment state, but before she knew it, she was entering the building twenty minutes early.

And also before she knew it, her finger had hit the fourth floor button.

He wasn't there. She knew because she stood outside the gym, eyeing each and every treadmill that lined the huge room, but she couldn't see him—

"Tessa."

She managed not to jump but did grimace before turning to face Reilly, who'd apparently just gotten off the elevator behind her. Up close and personal, after a three-day break, he was even taller, darker and...hotter than she remembered. "Hi."

He nodded toward the gym. "You going to work out?"

She nearly laughed, except she was sure it would sound half-hysterical so she swallowed it. "Um, no."

"You get off on the wrong floor?"

"No."

"Oh. Are you...looking for me?"

She sighed and forced herself to look in his eyes and not at his leanly muscled athletic body. "Do you remember my claim that I wasn't pathetic with the opposite sex?"

"I remember," he said.

"Well, scratch that."

Was that a smile lurking around his mouth? Because if it was, she was going to slug him. "I'm quite pathetic," she said. "Just so you know." And she moved around him toward the elevator, punching the up button with far more force than was strictly necessary.

"Did Eddie call you this morning?"

She waited for the elevator while staring at the closed doors, wondering if she could have possibly made a bigger fool of herself. "Yes."

"He won't give me Marge back."

"I'm sorry."

She heard his soft oath, then felt his hand on her arm as he tugged her around. "Look, it's not what you think," he said.

"Really? And what do I think, Reilly?"

"I don't know..." He shoved his fingers through his already-standing-straight-up hair. "That I don't want you here, that I'd rather have Marge."

"Wow. Did you figure that out all by yourself?" She punched the up button again for good measure.

"Look, I'm trying to apologize for you getting manipulated into this job for another week," he said. "Eddie has a way of getting what he wants, at any cost."

"I don't need an apology from you." And she was sad to think he thought she did. "I..." Horrified to find her throat tight and her eyes burning, she inhaled slowly, but it didn't help. Nothing would. "I just...like the work," she whispered.

Thankfully the elevator opened and, yanking her arm free, she stepped onto it.

Quickly, she punched the fifth floor button, then, because he was still standing there in his work-out clothes staring at her as if she were a mixture of a cross he had to bear and a morsel he'd like to nibble on, she hit the close door button as well.

The doors slowly, way too slowly, started to slide together—

Until he slapped his hand inside. The doors shuddered, then opened again. "Tessa."

Oh, no. She was done talking. She hit the close door button with renewed vigor, and watched through shimmering vision as it started to close.

"Damn it." This time he shoved his broad shoulders through the doors and stepped on with her.

Fine. She'd just get off. She punched the open door button.

But he punched the close door button.

The doors closed and she reached for the control panel yet again, but Reilly grabbed her wrist—

Just as the elevator suddenly jerked so forcibly they both stumbled. The doors stayed closed.

The alarm went off.

"Look what you've done," Tessa said, shaking her head. "Now we're stuck."

"What *I've* done?" He dropped her wrist and turned to the control panel again. "There must be something—"

The alarm silenced abruptly and then the phone on the panel rang. Reilly answered it and listened for a moment. When he hung up, he looked at her.

"Well?" she demanded. "What did they say?"

"That I shouldn't ride in elevators with a crazy woman."

She rolled her eyes.

"They said it'd be just a few minutes."

She crossed her arms over herself and wished she'd stopped for doughnuts.

"Cold?"

She didn't answer. She would not be charmed by his concern, because the man didn't *feel* concern. He felt nothing. His feigned beta-ness was just that—feigned.

"Tess?" Shocking her, he moved closer, put his big, warm hands on her, and with that sinfully light touch he had, ran them up and down her arms.

"I'm not cold," she whispered, but in direct opposition to the words stepped just a little closer so that her heels and his athletic shoes were touching. She kept her head down and absorbed his caress.

"I want you here," he said after a long minute. "I really want you here."

She lifted her head and stared at him, stared into his direct and beautiful light-blue eyes. "Why didn't you just say so?"

He let out a long breath. "I didn't intend to say it now, but you looked so..."

"Pathetic?"

"No." He kept touching her. "I really do want you here," he repeated. "I'm sorry I didn't say it sooner, but..."

"But...?"

"But I think I just realized it."

He'd just realized it. She thought about that and about how she felt. *She'd* realized from the very start that she was attracted to him, that it was a dangerous sort of an attraction, but an attraction nevertheless.

But she supposed that's the kind of woman she was—impulsive. She acted first, thought later. Just as she could accept that, she could also accept that he was different. He had a much more methodical, linear way of thinking. It easily could have taken him all week to realize what she'd understood in five seconds that night at Eddie's.

Certainly standing as close to him as she was, she could feel his "attraction," but that was a purely physical response. She knew he probably didn't feel much more than that and, in all likelihood, he might never feel more than that.

Hence the danger.

"So will you stay the week?"

Her heart sighed. "I'll stay the week."

"And you won't get us stuck in an elevator again?"

"If you'll..."

"What?" he murmured.

Kiss me.

"Tess?"

She gave him a smile through the ache in her heart. "Nothing." She turned away and studied the control panel. "Think our few minutes are almost up?"

Once again, his hands settled on her hips as he turned her to face him. Slowly he drew her close.

"What are you doing?"

"With you, Tess, I swear I never know."

She put him off-kilter. Perversely, she was glad and slid her arms around his neck. "Never?"

"Well..." He looked at her mouth.

And because she couldn't help herself, she closed the gap and put her mouth to his.

A rough groan rumbled from deep in his chest. His hands slid up her arms to cup her head, which he held in place. As if she was going anywhere! As before, the very connection kick-started her pulse. His mouth was warm, firm and didn't have to work at all to coax hers open. In less than two seconds, they were glued together, bodies straining, hands fighting for purchase. Tessa could hear the little whimpers for more coming from deep in her throat and, if he hadn't let out a ragged groan and pressed her back against the wall for better leverage, she might have been horrified at herself at how far gone she was, but at least he was just as far gone.

When he finally pulled back, his breathing as ragged as hers, she put a hand to her fluttering belly and cleared her throat. "Was that work-related?"

He frowned and said, "What? No."

"Just checking." She tugged his head back to hers. "You see?" she whispered, her mouth a fraction of an inch from his. "It's not all about work—"

"Tess—"

She kissed him again. And then again, before he took over. He had a thigh insinuated between hers and his hands were busy making her body hum when suddenly the elevator jerked and started moving.

It was over.

Feeling overcharged and sensitized, Tessa blinked when the doors opened on the fifth floor to reveal Reilly's office just the way she'd seen it last.

Everything looked so...normal.

In a bit of a fog—no doubt, a sexual one—she stepped off and felt Reilly do the same behind her.

She turned and looked at him. Other than wearing his work-out clothes, he looked the same as always. In cool, tight control.

"What?" he asked.

Slowly she shook her head. Damn it, she'd broken her vow. *She'd* kissed *him*. And now her nipples were hard and achy, straining against her blouse. Between her legs she was hot and damp. One more touch, she thought, and she just might implode on contact.

And he was standing there as if nothing had happened.

If that didn't put it all into perspective.... She forced herself to move as calmly as he did toward the front desk, and then pretended to bury herself in work.

And marveled at his ability to do it for real.

13

AS TESSA LEFT for work the next morning, her sister popped her head out of her door and made a big show of checking her watch. "Hmm."

Tessa rolled her eyes. "Don't start."

"Your car is working again so I wonder why you're leaving so early." She eyed Tessa's sleeveless purple blouse and cream skirt. "Let me guess, you're wearing the purple lingerie today?"

"Maybe I'm not wearing any."

Carolyn's mouth fell open and Tessa laughed. "Don't you have something else to do other than speculate on what I might or might not be wearing?"

"Sure. I can speculate on whether you might or might not get hurt. Who is this guy who's making you glow? Eddie's son? Reilly? I want to meet him. Rafe asked me about him, too."

Because when Rafe had called Tessa the night before, she wouldn't tell him anything either. "Nobody's making me glow except for this chilly morning." But she relented and kissed Carolyn. "Now, go have a good day, one that doesn't include obsessing about my life." She got to the carport and slid into her car. She patted the dashboard as she did every morning. "Good girl," she coaxed and turned the key.

Nothing.

This was not happening. She shook her head and tried again. And then again, and finally had to concede she needed a new car. A new *used* car.

As was becoming routine by now, she took the bus, glancing at her watch every three seconds. She was still plenty early, and if she ran the block from the bus stop to the office...

Reilly was on a different treadmill this morning, looking long and hard and sleek and damp. Tessa sagged back against the wall, breathless from both the run and the view.

"Can I help you?" asked a woman dressed in white work-out shorts and a green polo shirt emblazoned with the logo of the gym.

Tessa jumped and straightened. "Um...no. Thanks." Guiltily, she got back on the elevator and fanned her face all the way up to the fifth floor.

Reilly came in shortly after, carrying a duffle bag that she knew held his clothes for the day, clothes he'd change into after his shower. And though he greeted her before he headed toward his office, he looked awfully tense for someone who'd just worked out. She waited a little while—imagining him in the hot water all wet and sleek and soapy—before she brought him some files she knew he needed.

"Thanks," he said and didn't look at her.

She moved to the door, then stalled. "Are you okay?"

"Sure." He was using his adding machine, his fingers racing over the keys.

So much for stalling. Still, she tried one more time. "Where's Cheri?"

"She's defected. She's helping out Eddie."

"And how is your father? Any more trouble?"

"No."

"Okay, then." She bit her lip, wondering how else to drag this out, but she had nothing.

Back at her desk, she worked for a few hours before she took a call from Eddie.

"Is my idiotic son there?"

"Well...yes."

"Is he sleeping at his desk?"

"Why would he do that?"

"Because the boy is burning the candle at both ends, that's why, babysitting me all night, then working all day."

"He said you were doing fine."

"Because he's making sure of it. He's always over here. I wanted some time with him, but this is ridiculous. Tell him to go home. Demand it."

"Eddie," she said, laughing, "have you ever had any luck demanding anything of Reilly?"

"Well, no." He laughed regretfully. "At least tell him I just heard from the police. They think Sheila's left the country. That means I'm safe. Oh, and tell him I promise not to date any more psychotics, so he can relax."

Tessa didn't think this was a conversation she wanted to deal with. "Why don't I just transfer you to him?"

"Because he'll listen to you. Look, whatever you do, just don't let him come to my house tonight, okay? He needs his rest. I'm going to be just fine."

"You're *sure?*"

"As much as it secretly thrills me that he cares enough to want to keep me safe," Eddie said, more serious than she'd ever heard him, "I'm completely positive. He can't go on like this, he just can't."

"And the police are certain—"

"Don't worry about me. Just keep Reilly from trying to babysit me again tonight." His voice softened. "Be patient with him, Tessa."

"Eddie, I can't just—"

A dial tone sounded in her ear. She pulled the phone away and stared at it. She was to keep Reilly from trying to babysit Eddie. Right! The man was sorely mistaken if he thought she had that kind of influence over his son.

No one did. Reilly was his own man, who came and went as he pleased. His own man who, in spite of himself, cared deeply about the people around him.

She thought that just might be the sexiest thing about him. Sexier than his alpha behavior—and she hated to admit just how sexy that was. Sexier than how hard he worked. Sexier than kissing him, and that was pretty damn sexy.

Glancing at the clock, she rose and hit the intercom button for Reilly's office. "I'll be right back," she said, and thought she heard a low, guttural grunt of a reply.

Well, no one would ever accuse him of talking too much, that was sure. A few minutes later she was back in the building, armed with takeout Chinese, her favorite. Heading straight down the hall, she let herself into Reilly's office.

He was so engrossed with his computer, he didn't move.

She came up behind him and dangled the bag between him and the computer screen. "Guess what time it is."

"I could tell by the scent coming down the hall."

So he *had* heard her coming. That shouldn't have surprised her; he had the finely honed senses of a warrior. "Let's go to the staff room," she suggested.

"I'm too swamped." But he put his computer to sleep and turned to face her as he rubbed his temples, looking so tired, she set the bag on the desk and touched his arm. "You look terrible, you know that?"

He let out a laugh and said, "Well, don't hold back. Just tell me what you're thinking."

"I always will," she said softly and kneeled before him, putting her hand on his knee. "Reilly? Why don't you go home early? Get some sleep."

"Why would I do that?"

"I don't know, maybe because you've been up how many nights in a row now, making sure your father is safe?"

His eyes went a little chilly. "That had to be done."

She sat back on her heels. "Wow, you're good at that."

"At what?"

"At shutting people down."

"I'm not shutting you down."

"No, you're shutting yourself down. Making sure you don't feel anything—not worry for Eddie, annoyance at Cheri, or...whatever for me."

"*Whatever* for you? What the hell does that mean?"

"We kissed in the elevator yesterday and you walked away like we'd shaken hands. You never felt a thing."

"What should I have felt, Tess?"

"You know what? Never mind. Be a non-feeling robot." She stood and moved to the door.

He stood, too. "What did you just call me?"

She turned back and said, "A non-feeling robot."

"You really think I don't feel?" he asked incredulously. He stalked the length of the office to stand toe-to-toe with her. "I have plenty of feelings, damn it."

She knew he did, just as she knew he hid them. She felt bad for upsetting him, but he'd asked for it. "Why don't you ever show any?"

"Maybe I don't like to exhibit everything I feel for show-and-tell."

"Right, because if you keep all your feelings inside, you can control them." She lifted her hands to cup his face. "That makes me sad, Reilly. Sad for you. You never vent. You never say how you feel about Cheri working for Eddie, though it clearly bothers you. You never say how you feel about what is happening to your father or what happened to us—"

"You think I don't feel anything about any of that?"

"Unless you tell me, how would I know?"

He stared at her.

"Look," she said, relenting. "I know some people have trouble getting in touch with their feelings. It's not easy, but you need to vent or—" She broke off when he picked up a file on his desk and flung it at the opposite wall, where it opened and rained papers down to the floor. "W-what was that?"

"A vent," he said roughly. "How was that?"

"Um..." She swallowed. "Good. Really...good."

"That's how I feel about what happened to us," he said. "That's how I feel about what happened to *you*." He grabbed her and she expected anger or maybe a hard, thorough kiss, but instead he put one light, gentle hand over her throat, where her bruises had started to fade, the other at the small of her back, nudging her closer.

Her entire body softened to fit his.

"If I could go back and erase that night, I would." His hands were soft and tender, his eyes utterly fierce.

"I'd like to make sure you never got hurt again. Are you getting how strongly I feel about that, Tess?"

She nodded and whispered, "Yes."

"Good." He pulled her hard against him, putting his mouth very close to hers. "I blame myself for that night. And I'm going to have to blame myself for this as well, as there's no one to point a finger at. I hate it when that happens."

And he closed his mouth over hers.

14

HE WAS KISSING HER, he was finally kissing her, fierce and demanding. Tessa gave it back to him, gave him all she had and when he came up for air, she couldn't help it, she bit his lower lip.

With an oath, he came back at her, his big hands holding her head still for another long, ravishing, deep kiss. It was amazing, it was earth-shattering and she literally shook with it, and yet she wanted to dance and shout.

He'd really kissed her. He'd really started it and frankly, she didn't intend to let him finish for a good long time. Lifting her hands, she ran them over his arms and shoulders and chest, but that wasn't enough, she needed more, so she pulled his shirt front from his trousers and slid her hands beneath to his chest, roaming over his hot, sleek flesh.

He sucked in a harsh breath and bent a little so he could band his arms more tightly around her. They stumbled then, back against his desk. A stack of files fell to the floor.

Laughing breathlessly they straightened away from the desk, landing with a thud against the opposite wall, where he pinned her for a long, blissful moment during which his hands slid beneath her blouse as well, cupping her breasts and teasing her nipples.

"One of these days," he growled, "I'm going to get you back into a bedroom. Yours, mine, I don't care."

With a rough sound of frustration, he undid her buttons, pulled both her blouse and bra down her arms and touched her skin-to-skin this time. Shivering, she dug her nails into his back while he dragged hot, wet, open-mouth kisses down her throat, taking special care with each and every still-visible mark on her. Only when he was done, silently paying homage to every inch, did he wander his way to her bare shoulder, then back up her collar bone, still licking, tasting, kissing.

It wasn't enough. Even as she thought it, he plumped up her breasts with his hands, driving her crazy with nothing more than his mouth. He didn't lift his head for a long time, and far before he did, Tessa's body came alive—glowing, aching, pulsing with pleasure and need and heat. She wanted to make wild, messy, mind-bending love right here in his office, she wanted—

"Tessa." Breathing heavily, he put his forehead to hers. His fingers went from making her writhe and whimper with pleasure to drawing slow, soothing circles on her back.

Not a good sign.

"This is not a smart idea," he said a little thickly.

Definitely not a good sign. "You have a lock on your office door," she managed to say.

He looked at the door, at the lock in question, and she could see him hesitate.

She didn't want him to hesitate. She wanted him naked.

"I have a client coming in at two." He leaned back to look at the clock.

Ten minutes until two.

She wanted to cry. Wanted to howl, and by the looks of him as he shoved his fingers through his hair, he felt the same way.

"We could go lock the glass doors," she said quickly. "And pretend you're not here—"

"Tess. I can't take you here, not like this. We need privacy." He slid her bra straps back up. The backs of his fingers brushed her pebbled nipples, ripping a shiver from her.

He groaned. "And *hours*," he said roughly. "We need lots of hours."

"I think I only need a minute."

He closed his eyes and murmured, "Don't make this harder." He slid his fingers into her hair and tilted her head up to his. Eyes still closed, he kissed her, one long, clinging kiss that made a soft, clingy noise that tugged between her thighs.

"Tess," he whispered, just that, just her name.

Her heart stumbled and she hugged him hard.

They heard the doors opening, signaling the arrival of his client and they stared at each other.

"I'll bring the files you need," she said, but didn't let go of him. "Thank you," she whispered.

"For what?"

"For showing me how you feel. I know it must have been hard."

He smiled ruefully and said, "Hard? You don't know the half of it." He shifted his hips against her, showing her what exactly was "hard," making her laugh softly as she pulled away.

MUCH LATER, long after he'd seen his client, Reilly surfaced from his computer and stretched, glancing at his clock.

Six-thirty.

He pushed away from his desk and went down the hall, wondering if—

No, Tess hadn't left without saying goodbye. She sat at the front desk, bent over a stack of papers, her hair falling into her eyes as she chewed on the eraser on her pencil and muttered to herself.

Just seeing her there made something within him soften and relax. "Hey," he said quietly, not wanting to startle her.

For the first time since he'd met her, she didn't jump. Instead, she craned her neck to give him a smile that was at once both sweet and unbearably sexy.

His gaze dropped to her mouth.

So did hers and she let out a little laugh that sounded just a tad unsure. That made two of them. "It's past quitting time," he said.

"I know."

"I appreciate all the extra work you've put in since Cheri's gone Benedict Arnold on me."

"You're going home, right?"

Ah. Now he got it. He'd babysat Eddie and now she was babysitting *him*. He moved around, turning off the stereo, pulling the shades, turning off most of the lights before moving toward the front desk to shut down the computer for the night.

One thing his life experiences had given him were heightened senses, whether he liked it or not. Even from across the room he could smell her, some complicated mix of soap and shampoo and lotion that probably hadn't been designed to drive him insane.

"Reilly?"

There was only the one light left, by the elevator doors, and the glow of it fell over her face as she moved to stand in front of him and put her hand on his arm. Her eyes were so incredibly green and so incredibly focused on him, he felt as if she could see all the way through him.

He liked to keep himself distant, he prided himself on it, and yet with her it was damned difficult. Even when he shut her out, which he'd done on purpose rather than cave in to what she made him feel, she didn't give up on him. He should probably tell her to, because he could tell she had hopes for him. He should just say right here, right now, for her not to bother.

Pinning hopes on him was just a waste of time.

"Are you going home?" she asked again.

He tucked a stray strand of hair behind her ear. He did it as an excuse to touch her, which was startling. "That's generally the idea behind leaving work."

She cocked her head and gave him a long look. "You're being evasive on purpose."

"Am I?"

"Yes. You're going to Eddie's. He said I needed to keep you from doing that. He said you needed to go home to bed, Reilly."

To bed. *With her?*

Something within him went hot at that thought. She blushed, letting him know that he was slipping, that he'd let that thought show. "Come on," he said. "I'll walk you out."

She grabbed her purse and they got on the elevator. She stared at the closed doors as they began to descend, then looked at him. "I'm sorry about earlier, when I said you didn't have any feelings. That was wrong of me."

The elevator doors opened into the lobby. There were only a few people milling around and no one close. He stopped her when she would have walked away. "I don't want you to be sorry."

"What do you want?" she asked.

He stared at her. Hell if he knew.

"It's okay," she whispered. She started walking away, counting change out of her purse.

"What are you doing?"

"Getting my bus fare ready."

His stomach did that slow somersault that only she could cause. "I thought your car was fixed."

"*Was* being the operative word, apparently."

"I'll give you a ride."

She looked up, then laughed softly. "Thanks, but don't worry. I'm off duty. I'm no longer your responsibility."

"I'm giving you a ride." And he took her hand to prove it, leading the way out of the building and toward his car.

"I know you'd rather be alone," Tessa said when they stopped by his car.

He unlocked his passenger-side door for her, waiting until she slid in before he leaned down and spoke, his mouth only an inch from hers. "Yeah, I want to be alone. Alone with *you*." It wasn't often he came right out and admitted such a thing to a woman and it had been a hell of a long time in any case. He expected a coy smile in return.

Or maybe mock shyness.

He didn't expect her to lift up enough to wrap her arms around his neck and kiss the very corner of his mouth before murmuring, "That makes two of us." Then her busy, hot little mouth worked its way to the other side of his for another nibble, keeping her eyes open on his the entire time. Slowly, purposely, she glided the tip of her tongue across the crease of his lips.

Hands shaking a little, he pulled back and put her seat belt on.

"Not here either, I suppose," she said with a little sigh, leaning back as she echoed his earlier words in his office.

"Tess—"

"I know. Probably not anywhere, right?" She sat back and slipped out of her sweater. When she leaned forward to tuck the sweater down by her purse, her sleeveless, scooped-neck blouse gaped open enough to reveal the very top curve of her breasts, and her purple silky bra.

"We work together," he said a little desperately. Did her panties match?

"Yep, we work together. We work and we obviously, as evident in your office earlier and also in the elevator a few days before that, do more."

He shut her door and came around the car, sliding in behind the wheel. "It's that 'more' that's holding me up."

"You don't like making love?"

He jerked his gaze to her, then concentrated on merging into traffic because looking at her, seeing her need and hunger reflected in her eyes, a need and hunger that matched his own, killed him. "I like...making love."

"Are you sure?"

Was he sure? The woman couldn't see he had an erection threatening the very zipper on his pants? "Very," he said tightly.

"Then what's the problem? I mean, we're attracted to each other, Reilly. Are you going to deny that?"

"No."

"We're also adults. So I don't see why—"

"Because you deserve more than what I can give you." He glanced over at her again. "Way more."

"I don't mean to sound contrary, but that's *my* decision."

His jaw started to twitch, a muscle reaction he hadn't had since leaving the CIA. He put his fingers to the spot and said, "I'm an in-the-present type of guy."

"What does that mean?"

"It means I can give you work. I can give you conversation. I can even give you great sex, but—"

"Great sex?"

She looked extremely intrigued. Damn it.

"How do you know for sure?" she asked. "Unless we try it..."

Oh man.

"Ah," she said, nodding. "I get it now. It was the L-word. I specifically said making love, didn't I. Well, I'll settle for wild, hot sex then. How about that, Reilly? Are you up for that?"

15

WAS HE UP for hot sex? Was she kidding? He was "up" all right. Reilly tried concentrating on the traffic, but for once there wasn't much. He glanced at Tessa, who was waiting for him to answer. "You realize we nearly simultaneously combust every time we touch."

She nodded. "Yes. Which I figure will come in handy in bed."

Restraint sorely tested, he gave up reasoning with her and just drove. They were within a few minutes of her place when his cell phone rang.

Eddie's number showed up on the display. "You get your wish," Reilly said into the phone in lieu of a greeting. "I'm staying away tonight." But he got no response to that, which was strange. Eddie had a response for everything. "Eddie?"

Still nothing. Not breathing, not a sound, nothing but a wide open connection.

With cool, calm precision, Reilly did a U-turn and got on the freeway northbound, heading toward La Canada. "Eddie," he said again.

Still nothing.

Tessa was looking at him. "What's the matter?"

A very bad feeling, for one. "Eddie," he said into the phone. "I'm going to call 9-1-1—"

"Reilly."

He nearly sagged in relief at the sound of his father's whispering voice, even though it came from far away, signaling that Eddie wasn't speaking into the phone at all, but at it. "Eddie, are you—"

"I can't hear you," Eddie whispered in an odd voice. "So I hope you can hear me. I dialed with my toes. I sure as hell hope you're there and that you haven't let some sweet young thing answer your phone for you. Wait, what am I saying, you don't even like sweet young things." He let out a little laugh. "Anyway, son, I'm in a bit of a bind, as you might have guessed. Literally. Don't call the cops," he said quickly. "You'll see why when you get here. You are getting here, aren't you?"

Reilly shook his head and pressed on the gas.

"I don't want you to get upset or anything," Eddie whispered, "but the police were wrong about Sheila. I'd call them myself and mention it, but...well, you'll see."

Reilly got off the freeway in La Canada and raced up Foothill Boulevard, going far above the speed limit.

Tessa's fingers gripped the console, but she said nothing about his driving. "Is he okay?"

"I'm not sure."

They turned onto Eddie's street, but instead of pulling into the driveway, Reilly turned off the engine and kept his cell phone to his ear. Most of the La Canada Foothills were covered with growth indigenous to the mountains of Southern California. Eddie's lot was no exception and the view of the house was blocked by tall, staggered oaks and pines. He turned to Tess. "Wait here."

She already had her hand on the handle of the door. "What's the matter?"

"I haven't a clue." Eddie had stopped talking, which was worrisome. "But given my father and his life, it could be anything." He pulled a gun from the glove box and glanced at Tessa when she gasped. He tucked the gun in the waistband of his trousers. "You have your cell phone on you?"

"Yes. Reilly—"

"If I'm not back in ten minutes, call the cops."

"*Reilly.*"

He looked into her shocked green eyes and saw pure stubbornness. She was going to be difficult about this. He shouldn't have been surprised. "Look, the call was just a bit strange, even for Eddie. Given what we've been through in this very house, humor me." He looked into her eyes, willing her to listen.

She nodded, then pulled out her cell phone and turned it on. "Ten minutes or call the police—" he said, breaking off when he leaned in for a quick, hard kiss he hadn't known he needed.

He pulled back and started to get out of the car.

"It's getting dark," she whispered, her hand grabbing the front of his shirt. "I know how you feel about the dark. Let me come with you."

She was going to kill him, this woman of the soft eyes and soft heart and the body that could bring him to his knees. "Wait here," he repeated, then got out of the car. He stepped off the sidewalk and into the thick grouping of trees as he made his way toward the house under the security of the growth, wondering what the hell he was walking into this time.

Darkness hadn't fallen yet, but it was close and no lights had been put on upstairs. In comparison, the downstairs blazed with lights, as well as the sounds of glass shattering and other assorted thumps and bumps that signified either a temper tantrum or that someone had decided to help his father redecorate in a very expensive manner.

Reilly skimmed around the back, keeping hidden by all the bush, which was easy enough to do. Damn, his father was extremely lax in the security department. In fact, this whole place, with the myriad of windows and doors—everything—it was all a virtual security nightmare.

The back door was unlocked. Naturally. Eddie might as well put out a sign that said *come screw me over, please.* Since no more commentary had come from his cell, he stuck it in his pocket. Then he pulled out his gun and entered. At the sound of more glass raining down, he flattened himself against the wall and looked around. He stood in a lanai that led to a large den, which opened into the great room. From there he'd be able to see the kitchen.

That's where the glass-crashing sounds were coming from. He entered the den and saw no one.

From the kitchen came a screech that sounded furious and frustrated. "Take that!" a woman screamed.

He took the safety off the gun and headed into the great room. He could see a woman in the kitchen systematically tossing every piece of china and glass from the cabinets with glee. Reilly didn't recognize the fortyish, tall, leggy blonde, though she had the usual look of one of Eddie's preferred women—blond, stacked and...hard.

"And take *that!*" she cried and dropped a vase that looked quite expensive. She stomped on it. "Take that, you son of a bitch! Everything in this place should have been mine, *would* have been mine, if you'd just fallen in love with me." Another vase hit the floor. She stomped on that, too. "Like I did with you!"

"Well," Reilly said. "That was your first mistake, falling in love with the bastard."

Her head came up and she stared at Reilly, at the gun pointed at her, and blinked. "How did you—" she said, blinking again. "You're not Eddie."

"Nope."

"You look just like the no-good, son of a bitch."

"I had some bad luck with the genes," he agreed.

She tossed back her blond hair. Slowly licked her lips. "Are you as good in bed as he is?"

"Step away from the counter and the island," he said. "Out into the open."

Her full red lips affected a pout, but she did as he said. "I knew I was going to get caught this time," she said.

"So, you're the one. You're the ex-girlfriend...Sheila, right?"

"*Ex*," she said, nearly spitting it out. "I hate that word. Look, you can put away the gun. I'm not dangerous or anything."

"I don't think so." With his free hand, he pulled out his cell again and called the police, even though Eddie had asked him not to. He no longer cared. While he punched in the numbers, he kept an eye on the woman he assumed was as crazy as she seemed.

His father sure could pick them.

When he hung up, she tried a sweet smile. "I just wanted to hurt the schmuck like he hurt me," she said. "He discarded me like...like week-old trash."

"Not to be contrary or anything," he said, "but Eddie discards all women like week-old trash."

A sound behind him had him taking a quick peek, because he didn't intend to be taken down by this crazy lady's thugs again. But instead of thugs, he saw Tessa.

And his mother.

Cheri smiled weakly and waggled her fingers at him. "Um, I need to break in here." She eyed the hard-looking blonde with interest, then the mess at their feet, and finally Reilly, still holding his gun on the woman. "Honey, is that really necessary?"

Reilly laughed in disbelief. "Yes, very necessary. Mom—"

"Eddie doesn't discard *all* women," Cheri said softly.

"He discarded you—"

She shook her head and made her way closer. "It's time I told you the truth, baby. Eddie never wanted me to tell you and I'm not sure if that was stubborn pride or misguided loyalty to me," she said, sighing, "but I discarded him. I was young and stupid and didn't want to be tied down." She shook her head and said, "And you want to hear the crazy truth? I've been regretting that decision ever since."

He stared at her. "And you're telling me this now because...?"

"I don't know," Cheri said, lifting a shoulder. "Because you're acting as if all your troubles are his fault."

Sheila laughed. "Listen, Mommy Dearest, why don't you take your boy's gun away and then turn your head, huh? And I'll just get the hell out of your hair."

Cheri lifted a brow. Checked out the mess once more. And slowly smiled.

Sheila did, too, in relief.

"Sorry," Cheri said, shaking her head. "You're going to jail, and you're never going to bother Eddie again."

Sheila's smile faded. She muttered, "Hell."

Sirens sounded in the distance.

Reilly looked at Tessa, who was standing there quietly. "What happened to waiting in the car?"

"I was, but then your mother pulled up and there was no stopping her," Tess said, smiling when Cheri put her arm around her shoulders. "I couldn't let her come in here alone."

Reilly looked around. "Where the hell is Eddie?" he asked.

Sheila laughed and the sound held enough evil that chills raced down Reilly's spine. He shoved the gun at Tessa and ordered, "Keep this pointed at her until the cops come in. Mom, go show them where we are."

"Got it," Cheri said and Reilly ran through the house looking for Eddie.

He found him in his bedroom, tied spread-eagle to the bed. Naked. Eddie had a rueful smile on his face and the phone off the hook near his toes. "Found her, did ya, son?"

Reilly let out a disgusted sound and started on the knots. "You're a case, you know that?" he said.

"I do."

Reilly got one foot free. "And you sure know how to pick 'em."

"Yeah." Oddly enough, he didn't say anything more, as if he was...embarrassed, which couldn't possibly be the case, since nothing embarrassed Eddie.

At least nothing Reilly could think of.

When his father's hands were free, he sat up, but not in time to catch the robe Reilly tossed him. It hit him in the face. Pulling it down, he said, sighing, "Look, Reilly, about tonight..."

Reilly was certain he did not want to hear this, but just as certain he was going to hear it anyway. "What about it?" he asked.

"I was thinking...maybe you could forget to mention this whole incident to your mother."

Reilly turned to face him and blinked at the genuine look of remorse on Eddie's face.

"It'd be a bit mortifying," Eddie admitted, "to find yourself at the mercy of a woman you don't want, in front of the woman you do."

"You...want Mom?"

"From the day I first saw her in gym class."

"But... All those other women—"

"Hey, I never claimed to be a saint. Besides, for years now she wouldn't give me the time of day. Playing around...it was a pretty fine way to pass the time when I thought she didn't want me. But you know what?"

Reilly was afraid to know, he really was.

Eddie arched a brow. "Lately, I've got the feeling I've got a shot with her. Unless, of course, she'd have seen me up here tonight. That might have sealed it for me, the wrong way."

The man truly *was* embarrassed, when Reilly would have bet his last dollar he'd have been laughing like hell over what had happened to him.

It didn't make sense until he thought about what his

mother had said, how *she'd* left Eddie and not the other way around as he'd always thought.

And wondered why that, in turn, softened him, just a little, when he didn't want to be softened. "So you're saying that you're not quite as smooth as you like everyone to think?"

"Oh, sure. Make me repeat it," Eddie sighed. "Please. Whatever you think of me, just don't tell her."

The man was completely, one-hundred percent serious. Even...earnest. Reilly shifted uncomfortably at the compassion that blindsided him. "I'd promise, but it's too late, Romeo. She's downstairs."

Eddie picked up his shirt and quickly shoved his arms in it.

Reilly sighed and tossed him his pants. "Hurry. Because... Dad?"

At the unaccustomed name, Eddie went still. Swallowed hard. "Yeah?"

"I won't tell her."

Reilly staggered back a step when Eddie hugged him hard, and then lifted his hands to hug his father back.

16

THE NIGHT WAS DARK and warm. There was no moon and being Los Angeles, the stars weren't that bright either, but there was just something about a summer night in Southern California that couldn't be beat.

Tessa put her hand on Reilly's when he turned off the engine of his car. They were parked in front of her apartment building and it was very late.

They'd had to stay for the police and then had started to help Eddie clean up his mess, at least until Cheri had softly ordered them to go.

When they'd left, Cheri had been helping Eddie, the two of them quiet. Not an uncomfortable quiet, but the silence of two people comfortable together.

They'd had a lot of time to get that comfortable, Tessa thought, looking at Reilly. Thirty-something years. And she could tell by the warm way the two of them had been looking at each other that maybe things were about to get even more comfortable tonight.

She hoped the same for her.

She didn't know what had happened between Reilly and Eddie in Eddie's bedroom, but whatever it had been, it had put Reilly in a quiet, pensive mood. "You okay?" she asked and squeezed his hand. "And I'm not looking for an 'I'm fine' here."

"But I am fine."

She had to laugh. He was such a guy. "Okay then."

Reilly looked at her and said, "How about this? When I'm not fine, I'll tell you."

That would have to do. Besides, he did look fine. He looked mighty fine. He looked she-wanted-to-see-him-naked fine.

She had no idea what had turned her into such a sexual creature lately, but knew he was a big part of it. She also knew he probably didn't want to hear that.

He walked her to her door, which she took as a good sign. Her last date had hardly slowed down the car enough for her to jump out.

She hadn't left any lights on and the porch was pitch-dark. She reached for his hand to show him the way, then unlocked and opened her door. Pushing it open she reached for the lights just inside and flipped them on. Then she turned on the living room lights and also her kitchen overhead, which illuminated her entire place in one fell swoop.

When she looked at him, he was shaking his head. He came close and cupped her face, a small smile curving his lips. "I'm not afraid of the dark," he said.

"What *are* you afraid of?" she whispered.

He was silent for a long moment. Then he replied, "Besides enclosed spaces and failing? Nothing."

"Nothing?"

"Well...maybe you. Maybe I'm afraid of you."

"I'm not that scary," she said, putting her hands over his. "I'm just a woman."

"Just a woman." He let out a rough laugh and put his forehead to hers. His hands went to her hips and squeezed before gliding up and down her back.

"I am." It was hard to think past the brush of his fingers. Tessa skimmed her hands up and over his shoulders, which she never got tired of touching because they were broad and hard with muscle. Then she slid her fingers into his hair, which was short and soft and, as usual, pretty much standing up on end. "I'm certainly not as scary as, say...working in the CIA."

He bent his head and put his face to her throat, letting out a breath that brought goose bumps to her skin. "You sure about that?"

She pressed closer and felt his body begin to react.

Her body was far ahead of him. "Pretty sure. At least I won't ever betray you and lock you in a trunk." She could smell his skin, feel the rumble of his voice and pressed even closer. "I'm not going to hurt you, Reilly, ever."

"Ah." His face still buried in her neck, he nodded and took a soft bite out of her flesh that made her knees wobble. "A promise that you can't possibly keep."

She tightened her fingers on his hair and lifted his head to look into his light-blue eyes that liked to hide behind a sheet of ice. "You don't like promises?"

At her back, his fingers slid beneath the material of her blouse. "I don't trust promises."

She knew he had a good reason to feel that way and her heart squeezed. "Well, how's this for one you can trust?" Unbelievably touched by this man and unbelievably turned-on, she wrapped him in her arms. He really was her man in black, still her superhero with the surprisingly soft center, her everything. She put her mouth to his ear and let out a slow breath, gratified to feel his arms tighten around her. "I promise to drive you wild tonight."

Another harsh laugh. "That's an easy one," he said. "You're doing it right now."

"Really?"

"Why so surprised?" he asked, arching his hips into hers. "Can't you tell?"

"Mmm-hmm." She kicked the door closed behind them and pressed her breasts to his chest. Oh, yes, she could feel his body's reaction and she arched into him even more, eliciting a low groan from deep in his throat. "How very interesting," she whispered.

"What?"

"You like me. You really like me."

Another groaning laugh. His fingers sank in her hair and he lightly tugged her head back, his eyes glittering into hers. "What are you trying to do, Tess?"

"If you don't know, then we have a problem."

"*Tess.*"

"Is it so wrong to give in to this heat between us tonight?" she wondered. "Is it?"

"Not if you mean it, that we're only giving in for tonight."

"I mean it," she confirmed. She would have liked to negotiate for more, but Reilly was who he was, and she had no desire to change him; she just wanted him to let her in. For tonight. She'd deal with the rest later. Leaning in she rimmed his ear with her tongue, then bit gently on the lobe.

Again his arms tightened on her and he sucked in a harsh breath. His heart beat heavily against her breasts and beneath her hands, she felt his hard, hot muscles tensing. "Did you figure it out yet, Reilly?"

"You're trying to seduce me."

"Is it working?"

He looked into her eyes for a long, heated beat. "Oh, yeah. It's working."

"Good." She had to remind herself that he wasn't her warm, compassionate beta man. He was dark and edgy and dangerous, not to mention unpredictable and not a safe bet for a soul mate.

But he tasted good and she wanted him and for tonight, for right this minute, it would be enough. She'd make it so. "Kiss me, Reilly."

"You took the thought right out of my head." Then his mouth opened on hers and he slipped his tongue inside to languidly slide against hers. She didn't fall to a boneless heap at his feet, but oh, she wanted to. Her fingers curled into his shirt and she held on for dear life as he delved deeper into her mouth.

It wasn't enough and she tugged at his shirt, pulling it over his head when he lifted his arms. When it went sailing across the room, she busied herself kissing all the broad, sleek flesh she'd exposed.

He let out a shuddering breath and pulled her blouse free from her skirt so he could stroke her bare ribs. His thumbs swirled over her belly button, delving a little lower to toy with the waistband of her skirt, even dipping beneath it to skim over her new purple panties. "Bedroom," he murmured thickly, and bent his knees a little to scoop her up in his arms.

"Wait."

He went utterly still and stared down into her face. "Wait?"

His entire body was taut with careful restraint and she could have hugged him—except she already was. "It's just that *I* was seducing you, and you've...sort of taken over. I want to do it, Reilly."

"You...want to do it?"

"Yes. So could you set me down? Please?" she added when he hesitated.

He set her down. "I took over," he repeated, sounding baffled.

"You do that a lot, actually." She took a deep breath because he was once again without a shirt and looked really...yummy. Not only did he look yummy, he looked hot and bothered and frustrated. She loved that look on him.

"Tess," he said, running a finger over her shoulder, then following that up with a kiss to the spot.

She wanted to melt again.

"You wanted to run the show here," he said. "Are you going to do that soon? Like maybe now?" he added hopefully when she just stood there absorbing his touch.

"Yes," she said, laughing, then swallowed her smile, straightened and got serious. "Pick me up."

His lips twitched. "Like I already had?"

"Yes."

Looking amused on top of hot and bothered now, he scooped her up against his chest and looked down at her, her big, alpha guy awaiting her instructions.

She flung her arms around his neck. "Couch," she commanded, ignoring his soft laugh, which turned into a groan when she bit his throat.

"I'm going to bite you back," he growled and tossed her on the couch.

She hadn't bounced once when his mouth found hers, hot and hungry while he unbuttoned her blouse, unhooked her bra and spread them away from her all in one movement. Before she caught her breath, a big, warm palm slid up the inside of her bare leg to touch her through her panties.

His gaze met hers as she arched into his hand. Pushing her skirt up to her waist, he slipped off her panties, then settled himself between her thighs, leaning in to kiss her again.

A little undone, she slapped a hand to his bare chest.

He let out a breath. "Not again. Too fast?"

"No. Fast is fine. It's just that you're doing that take-over thing again."

He let out a disbelieving laugh. "I'm at the good part and you want to discuss my take-over tendencies? *Now?*"

She smiled because he looked so...bewildered. "Yes."

With a long-suffering sigh, he came up on his knees and lifted his hands in surrender. "Okay. Go ahead. You take over."

"Lose the pants."

"Gladly." He wrenched himself away from her and got off the couch. The rasp of his zipper seemed extraordinarily loud. Looking down at her, he slowly stripped off his shoes, socks, pants and underwear and stepped free, holding something he'd taken from his pocket.

A condom.

And then just stood there, larger-than-life in her small living room, the contours of his hard body revealed by the lights she'd turned on earlier.

Definitely larger than life, *all* of him. She could have just looked at him forever, but he shifted restlessly and gave her a look that seared.

"You're so beautiful, Reilly."

He moved toward her with sexual intent blazing from his eyes, but when he reached the couch, he paused, fists clenched at his sides. "What now?"

He was trying to let her be in charge, trying, but not quite succeeding, and emotion swamped her. "Come here," she whispered and when she opened her arms, he settled himself back between her legs. He felt so good, so warm and strong. She wanted him, all of him, and she dug her fingers into his tight bottom, trying to push him in.

He laughed softly. "Where's the verbal instructions?"

"*Hurry.*"

"Now there's a good one." His hands tightened on her. She felt his mouth on her breasts, her belly, her thighs...and then in between. "Like this?" he murmured.

She let out a sort of strangled squeak that sounded horrifyingly needy. But she *was* horrifyingly needy. Her muscles were shaking, her everything was shaking and it wasn't anything like the short, vaguely pleasurable experience she'd expected, but more—so much, much more.

"Tess?" He kissed the inside of her thigh before lifting his head. "What's next?"

"Um..." She couldn't remember what she'd planned.

With a knowing smile, he dipped his head and licked her like a lollipop. She arched right into his mouth.

"Oh, wait," he said. "You didn't say to do that."

As if she was in charge at the moment. Ha! She'd never been in charge. But now he was looking at her, waiting, his eyes blazing. "More?" he asked politely.

"Yes." Her fingers tightened fiercely in his hair. "In fact, if you stop, I might kill you."

"Well, then." And he bent his head again and sucked her exquisitely sensitive little center right into his mouth.

She exploded on impact, saw fireworks, heard the explosion, felt the tremors, everything. When she could breathe again, Reilly was still between her legs, ready to sink into her, but she managed to slap a hand to his hard chest. "Wait."

His face was a mask of pleasured pain. "Again?" His voice sounded a bit strangled. He had a hand wrapped around his erection, holding himself poised at the juncture between her thighs and didn't look predisposed to play anymore.

She sat up. Somehow she managed to reverse their positions, pushing him down on his back. Leaning over him, she decided he was the most beautiful creature she'd ever seen. And he was all hers.

At least for tonight.

She kissed his chest, his belly and then, just as he had, she lay between his legs. "Hold still," she said. "I want to try..." And again, just as he had, she licked him.

At the guttural sound that escaped him, she looked up. "Problem?" she asked.

"Hell, yes." His jaw was granite, as was the rest of him. "I haven't..." He swore. "It's...been a while."

Her entire heart softened. "I know."

"Do you? Because one more touch from you and it's going to be over."

"Then we'll start again."

He let out a laughing groan that broke off in another groan when she took him into her mouth and suddenly, he was no longer laughing. When she swirled her tongue over the tip of him, he swore, then reached up and grabbed her, flipping her onto her back. He put on the condom, took her hands in his, stretched them up over her head and insinuated himself between her legs.

"Reilly—"

He covered her mouth with his and plunged inside her. "Sorry," he said, looking anything but, and pulled back only to thrust in again. And then again.

He'd taken over, driven by passion, passion for her, and it was the most thrilling experience of her life, making a man like Reilly want her so badly that he'd given himself completely over to her.

"Wrap your legs around me," he directed. "Yeah, like that— Tess..."

The way he said her name, the look on his face as he bent close to kiss her again, a hot, hard, demanding kiss that mimicked what the rest of his body was doing, all combined, taking her out of herself and when he whispered her name, she started shuddering again. In her arms, his muscles went taut, and he buried his face in her throat as he found his own release, which only extended hers, taking her to a place she'd never been. Taking them both.

IT'D BEEN A HELL of a long time since someone had knocked Reilly so completely for a loop, but Tessa had done it, she'd really done it.

At some point, they'd gone from the couch to the floor, though he'd rolled onto his back so he wouldn't suffocate her. He was still panting for breath, but he felt something else besides breathless. He felt a sharp tightness in his chest and he realized it had been there ever since she'd shown up in Eddie's house that night they'd been held up.

Maybe the funny tightness was stress. But whatever it was, he sure as hell didn't want to examine it too closely. Instead, he concentrated on drawing air into his lungs. No sooner than his heart had come down to anything close to resembling normal, Tessa's head popped into view.

With her hands all over him, she grinned. "That was fun."

"Fun," he concurred, nodding. Fun. "You nearly killed me."

"Really? I'm sorry."

He studied her flushed cheeks, her glowing eyes,

that I'm-quite-tickled-with-myself smile and had to laugh. "Yeah. You look real sorry."

"I am. Especially if I wore you out, because I was hoping..." Leaning in, she whispered what she was hoping.

It made him hard again.

"But if you're too tired..." She curled into his body, her hands still all over him. With a sigh, she set her head on his chest. "It's okay, if you are. We can just lie here."

Too tired? Not likely.

"I just want to be with you," she whispered and, head on his chest, let out a soft, happy sigh. "Just for tonight, Reilly. Isn't this nice?" She ran her fingers down his arm, his chest and belly. Over and over again, that soft, light touch.

He didn't have to look into her eyes to see she was giving him everything she had. That was the kind of woman she was. She had no idea how to hold back and even if she did, he doubted she'd ever even try. It made his heart ache, physically ache.

"Does this feel good?" she whispered.

He was completely hard again and knew she could see that he was. "Yes."

"You make me feel good, too, Reilly, just by being here. You can make me feel good by just looking at me."

He had no idea what to say to that, but she didn't seem to need a response. Slowly, her fingers stroked him and he let her. Her touch felt so good, so beyond what he'd expected or even wanted.

"Reilly?" She was breathless now and when he lifted his head, he saw her looking at his body and its reaction to her.

"Again?" she whispered hopefully.

"Again," he agreed and took her in his arms. "But next time, we make it to a damn bed." He started kissing her, letting himself get lost in the feel of her, the taste of her, but even that wasn't enough to obliterate the fact that this had not been some normal casual-sex thing.

Still wasn't. It was more, far more and damned if he could even begin to explain why.

So he didn't even try; instead, he bent to the task at hand, and took them both to heights of pleasure he'd never known before her.

17

EDDIE LAY IN HIS BED as the sun rose and held the love of his life.

Cheri stirred and opened her eyes. "Hmm," she said, and sat up. Fluffing her pillow behind her, she sighed. "I know that look. You're thinking too much. Regrets already?"

"Are you kidding?" He nearly laughed, but this wasn't a laughing matter. "I've never been happier."

"Me, either," she said, smiling. "Sorry it took me so long to come to my senses."

"That's okay. What's thirty-odd years between soul mates? I love you, Cheri."

"Oh, Eddie. I love you, too. So much." She stroked his jaw. "So, if we're okay..."

"I don't know about you, but I'm more than okay."

Cheri laughed and said, "All I'm asking is, what's the frown about?"

"Reilly."

"Ah." She let out a long breath as she continued to stroke him. "You're going to meddle, aren't you?"

"Of course I'm going to meddle. It's what I do best."

"Eddie—"

"No. I've got a good plan this time. Listen," he said. And he leaned in close, tugging the sheet free of her gloriously nude body as he did, whispering his plans as he made love to her again.

"What do you think?" he asked her when they could talk.

Glowing, Cheri sighed. "You know what? Color me crazy, but I think it just might work..."

WHEN TESSA WOKE UP, she was alone. That is, she was alone until her sister flipped on her bedroom light after she let herself in and, as she tended to do several times a week, went straight for Tessa's closet. "Do you still have my denim skirt?" Oblivious, Carolyn flipped through the hangers, then whirled around to dig her way through the clothes heaped on the chair next to the dresser. "I wish you'd return the stuff you take— Damn it, here it is. Is it even clean?" she asked, lifting the skirt. She shook it out, then lifted it up again.

She finally seemed to notice Tessa lying silently in her bed. "What's the matter?" she demanded.

What was the matter? Tessa took stock of her situation. Her entire body was warm and replete and deliciously sated. Not bad. The only thing missing was the fact that Reilly had clearly let himself out, probably shortly after their last tryst in the shower, sometime near dawn.

"Tessa," her sister said and stood by the bed now,

her hands on her hips. "Why aren't you saying anything?"

"Still sleepy, I guess." Tessa started to get out of the bed, but remembered she was quite naked.

Carolyn narrowed her eyes. "You're going to be late for work, aren't you?"

Somehow she didn't think Reilly would mind. Unable to get up until Carolyn left, she held the sheet up to her chin. "I think I'll just snooze another few minutes," she said.

Carolyn sighed. "Suit yourself. But I left you breakfast in the kitchen."

"You didn't have to do that."

"It's just yogurt and a bagel. Figured I'd save your cholesterol intake today, so you can skip the doughnut shop. Come on, come eat with me—" She tugged the sheet free of her sister's grasp and gaped. "Since when did you start sleeping in your birthday suit?"

Tessa scooped the blanket back up to her chin. "It was hot last night."

"It was sixty degrees."

"Well, it was hot in here."

"Uh-huh. And I suppose you bit yourself on your shoulder."

Tessa felt herself blush.

"Oh my God," Carolyn gasped, her mouth falling open. "You slept with him, didn't you? I hope to hell you used a condom."

"I'm not stupid." Tessa bit her lip. There had been no

sleeping involved, not even a bed. Nope, they'd used the couch, the floor, her table... "But it was really nice. You know, in case you were wondering."

Her sister sighed and sank to the bed. She skimmed a strand of hair out of Tessa's face. "You really like him."

"Yes."

"I want to meet him."

"I don't think it'll be happening again, Carolyn."

"Why?" Carolyn snapped. Her expression went fierce. "He doesn't like you?"

"He isn't much on commitment."

"Of course not. He's got a penis, doesn't he? Oh, sweetie." She leaned in and hugged Tessa. "Just don't let him break your heart." She pulled back and smiled grimly. "Because if he does, I'll break him."

Tessa laughed and said, "He's an ex-CIA operative. He probably knows twelve-billion different ways to kill a person."

"I don't need twelve-billion, not if he hurts you," she asserted. Carolyn stood and made her way to the bedroom door. "Feel free to tell him that. And what I can't accomplish, you know damn well Rafe will."

Tessa listened to the front door shut and had to shake her head. Love was an awfully strange creature. Carolyn loved Tessa, so she bossed her around and threatened people she didn't even know. Eddie loved Reilly so he interfered in his life. Cheri loved Reilly so she worked for him even though she'd rather work for Eddie. Sacrifices. All in the name of a four-letter word.

Love.

If she'd truly done as she was beginning to suspect, if she'd truly started to fall for Reilly...then what sacrifices would *she* make?

And would she be happy with those sacrifices, especially if she was the only one to make them?

With her sister gone, she got out of bed and showered. She was sore in places she hadn't imagined and besides the mark on her shoulder, there was an interesting one she didn't remember getting on the inside of her thigh.

For some idiotic reason, it made her grin.

When she got into work, Cheri was behind the front desk taking a phone message. When she hung up, she looked Tessa over until she wanted to squirm. "You okay?"

"Why wouldn't I be?" Tessa asked.

"Well, my son came in here in a decent mood. You have anything to do with that?"

Tessa bit her lower lip. "Maybe," she admitted.

Cheri nodded. "Good," she said, lifting some files. "Here's your work for the day. I have to run out for a few."

Tessa had started in on her work before she saw Reilly. He stopped by her desk and just looked at her.

She set down her pencil. "Hey."

"You okay?"

"You know, you're the second person to ask me that today."

His eyes never left hers. "Really? And what's the answer?"

"Are you asking because we got a little wild last night?"

"Yes."

She carefully shut her files. "Do I look that fragile, Reilly? That a few orgasms should have me falling apart?"

He craned his neck to see if Cheri was anywhere close.

"She took a break. We're alone."

"Good." He pulled Tessa out of her chair and down the hall to his office.

"Reilly, what—"

Through his office, stopping only to lock it, then past his desk to the attached bathroom. He locked that door, too. The small room was black and white and she could smell his soap from when he'd showered after his morning run. "You're driving me crazy," he muttered and pressed her against the counter.

She let out a little laugh. "I didn't do anything," she said.

"You said orgasms and it put a picture in my head of you panting my name as you came."

Her legs wobbled. Her nipples hardened.

He noticed. He made a rough, satisfied sound and

slid his arms around her, down the backs of her legs and up again, beneath her dress now.

She closed her eyes. "You could have stayed with me until morning. You could have—"

"Should have," he agreed, whispering her name, then his mouth covered hers as a slow burn took root in her belly. Her body fit itself to his in a desperate attempt to capture some of what they'd experienced last night.

She wore a sleeveless dress with a sweater over it. He tugged off her sweater and unzipped her dress, letting it pool in a heap at her feet.

She opened his pants and slid her hands inside, helpless to keep them off him. Once she touched him she couldn't think of anything else. He was hard, needing release and she was more than willing to give it.

Her bra and panties fell away and they were both lost then. He lifted her to the counter while she tore at his shirt and opened her mouth on his bare chest. He thrust into her and she arched back, taking more of him, taking all of him. He thrust again, and again, until, with a surprised cry, she came. Vaguely she heard his long, guttural moan as he followed her over the edge, but mostly all she could do was hold on and ride it out.

After what might have been an hour or just a moment, Reilly lifted his head from the crook of her neck. "What the hell was that?"

"Our bodies saying good morning, I guess." She slid

off the counter. "Don't look now but I think they like each other."

He laughed. *Laughed.* "That's an understatement."

She went still and looked at him as he reached for his shirt. What was he saying? That it was more than like for him?

Even...*love?*

But as he pulled on his shirt and tossed her panties at her, he gave no indication of such a thing. Not a single sign.

"A bedroom," he said softly, and kissed her again. "Next time, a damn bedroom."

She just stared at him, confused. He smiled at her and she managed a smile back. As she went to leave his bathroom, he reached for her, cupping her face, giving her a soft, clinging kiss before letting her go, a kiss she'd never forget.

THE NEXT MORNING Tessa was dressing for work when the phone rang. It was Eddie.

"I've got a favor to ask," he said. "I've got a client who needs a bookkeeper. It's confidential stuff and he doesn't trust anyone but me to send him the best and you're my best, Tessa. You interested?"

"Oh," she said. This caught her off guard. "But I still have today and tomorrow left at Reilly's, and—"

"Yes, well, I know that's been a terrible burden for you, working for my son. It was wrong of me to ask you to do it, so I figure this is a way to repay you. This new job will double your salary, plus it'll give you the one thing you asked me for when you first signed with me."

"What's that?" She couldn't think past one thought—she wasn't going to be working with Reilly anymore.

It didn't matter. It wasn't like they couldn't still see each other if they chose. And she chose.

But would *he?*

Would he want to continue what they'd begun? Given the heat they generated, given how he touched her, held her, she'd say yes, he'd definitely be interested in continuing their physical relationship.

But it would just be physical. If he felt more than that—which she suspected he did every bit as much as she did—he wouldn't want to face it, much less admit it.

"You wanted to travel," Eddie said. "You wanted adventure. I think this job'll fit the bill, as it's on a yacht in the Greek Islands."

She sank back to her bed. *"What?"*

"It's a three-month job and I just know you're going to have the time of your life."

Tessa went still. "Three months? In the Greek Islands?"

"My old friend is a world traveler. He's currently cruising the Greek Islands with his financial business right on board with him. Isn't it exciting?"

My God. Exciting didn't begin to explain it. But—

"This will kill two birds with one stone," Eddie said. "It'll get Reilly back his favorite temp, Marge, and you'll get what you wanted as well. Perfect, don't you agree?"

"Perfect," she agreed softly.

"CAROLYN." TESSA SHOOK her sister, then plopped on her bed. "Wake up."

Carolyn yawned. "Just take what you need from my closet. *Quietly*."

"I've got the choice between the Greek Islands for three months or staying and making a complete fool of myself over Reilly."

Carolyn's eyes flew open. "Come again?" she queried.

Tessa sighed. "Greek Islands, or Greek god in my bed."

"Some choice. Tell me about the paying option."

"Eddie's got a job for me on a yacht. But..."

"But... Don't tell me that but is Reilly." Carolyn sat up, looked into Tessa's face and sighed. "It's Reilly."

Tessa smiled, too. "Yeah," she admitted.

"So, I have to pick between some exotic water disease or a man I'm sure isn't good enough for you?"

That caused Tessa's first good laugh. "Yes, but remember, it's *my* decision."

Her sister nodded, looking amused and asked, "Then why are you here asking me?"

"Um..." Good point.

"Well, I vote for neither, if you're still asking."

"You know what? I'm not." Tessa hugged her sister hard. "But thank you," she whispered. "Thank you for always being there for me."

"Wait!" Carolyn called when Tessa headed to the door. "Which is it going to be?"

If only she knew. "I'll let you know."

"Tessa! Come back here. Mom and I were talking and we decided you should go to work for Dad! He promises you an annual two-week vacation, sick days and health insurance—"

Tessa gently shut the door. She'd handle this, on her own. She'd surprise everyone.

Even herself.

REILLY GOT OFF the elevator. He was early, so he was surprised to see Cheri's sweater hanging on the coat-rack.

She came down the hall and smiled at him.

"How nice to see you two days in a row," he said with just a hint of sarcasm. "Eddie didn't need you to-day?"

"No, but that reminds me. I wanted to tell you I'm going to date your father."

"You're going to...why?"

"I think he's cute."

Reilly shook his head. "You're crazy, you know that?"

"Yep." Cheri eyed him up and down. "Hmm."

Oh good Lord. He hated the *hmm*. "What?"

"Well, don't look now, but you actually resemble a normal person. A...happy person."

"Yeah. I'm happy. I'm happy you showed up for two days running."

"Uh-huh," Cheri said. She crossed her arms and leaned back. "Want to know what I think?"

He let out a long breath. "If I say no, will you go away?"

"I think you've been having sex."

"*Mom*." He covered his ears.

She laughed. "Well, it's about damn time. Isn't it amazing what getting a little will do for the soul?"

There hadn't been anything "little" about what he and Tessa had shared.

"You going to see her again?"

"Who?"

"Who," she said. His mother threw up her hands. "You know what? Don't even talk to me."

"*You* were talking to *me*."

"Well, I'm sorry I did." She started to go by him, then apparently changed her mind and waggled her finger in his face. "You know what your problem is?"

"Uh..." He stopped. "Is that a trick question?"

"You think in black and white, that's the problem. Well, guess what, Reilly? Life doesn't come in those colors. *Love* doesn't come in those colors."

"Mom, honest to God, you're making no sense."

"And furthermore, if you think you can make the

same mistake I did and ignore what's in your heart for thirty-something years, think again. It's a stupid thing to do, do you hear me?''

He let out a disparaging sound. "It was one night."

And a bathroom.

He'd never look at his Corinthian tile in the same way again. In fact, he'd been wondering if today they could try the storage closet...

"Oh, sweetie. Listen, I know you've been hurt before," Cheri said, touching his face. "God, I know it. And I've watched you close yourself off, I've watched you retreat, and it's killed me. But you're so brave, so strong. Surely, a man like yourself knows the wisdom of trying again."

"Mom—"

"You can't possibly believe you only get one shot at love—"

"Mom—"

"Don't fool yourself," she whispered. "Please don't. Tessa isn't like Loralee. She isn't."

Well, she was right about one thing. Tessa *was* different. First of all, she wasn't a cold-blooded killer. But more than that, she wasn't a one-night sort of woman and that was a problem. If they continued on, he would hurt her that way, when hurting her was the last thing he ever wanted to do.

But she wasn't the one for him, she was too cheery, too happy, too...everything that made his heart sing. He didn't want to do it. Not because of her, but because there was no *one* woman for him anymore, there just couldn't be—

The elevator dinged and off came Tess. She came through the glass doors and it took him a moment to figure out what was wrong. She was without her customary bright morning smile.

"Hi," she said nervously.

Nervously?

"Eddie called me this morning. Oh, here—" she said. She set a box of Krispy Kreme doughnuts on the front desk. "I bought you two days' worth."

Cheri divided a glance between her and Reilly, before moving down the hall. "I'll just give you two a moment alone."

"Why do we need a moment?" Reilly asked, a very bad feeling filling his belly. He turned back to Tessa. "And why did you buy *two* days worth of doughnuts?"

"Because I'm not working here anymore," Tessa said quietly. "Marge should be arriving any sec—"

The elevator dinged again and when the doors opened, Marge walked off. She was a large woman with prematurely gray hair ruthlessly twisted on her head, small wire glasses high on her nose and, in Reilly's experience, a perpetual frown on her face.

Only a few weeks ago, he'd thought she was the greatest thing since sliced bread. She worked hard, spoke to him only if necessary and never, ever looked so sexy he couldn't work, couldn't think, couldn't do any damn thing except drag her into his office bathroom.

She came through the glass doors and nodded to him, then tossed her purse on the front desk and sat behind it.

"What are you doing?" he asked her.

"What I always do when you need a temp. Looking for the files you leave out for me to do."

"But—"

Tessa put a hand on his arm. "That's what I'm trying to tell you. You've got your wish. Eddie brought Marge back," she said.

They both looked at Marge.

Marge stared back at them.

"Eddie called me this morning," Tessa said to him. "He's sending me on another job. Goodbye, Reilly."

And then, unbelievably, she started walking back toward the glass doors.

"Wait." He shook his head to clear it, but she was still walking away from him. Lunging forward, he grabbed her hand. "What did you just say?"

"Oh, Reilly. I'll never forget you," she murmured and touched his face. "I had a great time."

She pulled free, then moved through the doors toward the elevator, which was still open. She stepped on and pushed the down button. Her eyes were suspiciously damp but she was smiling when she turned back to wave. "Bye. Good luck."

But...that sounded like a very *final* goodbye. Even

if—and he couldn't believe his father had done this—
she wasn't going to work for him anymore, that didn't
mean they couldn't see each other. Right?

And in any case, he *wanted* her to work for him. He
wanted those cheery smiles. He wanted to hear her talk
and sing and laugh.

He wanted...her.

Damn it.

The elevator doors closed. And just like that, she was
gone.

He whipped around and stared at Marge.

She stared right back, still not a smile in sight.

He knew Marge never smiled at work. She didn't
sing either. In fact, she often turned off the stereo on
him. She often left the shades closed.

And she hated doughnuts. Now that he thought
about it, that was practically sacrilegious in itself.

"Where are today's files?" she asked, no-nonsense.
Nope, no dallying for this woman.

She'd done a great job for him for a long time. She always came through when he needed her and she was a
wonderful worker, but...

She wasn't Tess.

And, he realized, it had nothing to do with work at
all and everything to do with the way his heart felt as if
it had just been ripped in two.

Having felt that feeling before, he braced for the cold
iciness to descend. Waited to feel...nothing.

It didn't happen.

Instead, he felt a bone-deep certainty that this time, if it went bad, he had no one to blame but himself.

He raced for the doors.

"Mr. Ledger?"

"Take the day off, Marge."

"Mr. Ledger!"

He waved, and even added a smile. "Go ahead, take it off on me. Go do something you normally wouldn't."

"Well," she said, blinking. Then for the first time in his presence, she smiled back. "You do the same, Mr. Ledger."

He planned on it.

18

TESSA WAS HALFWAY to her car, halfway to a nice pity-party meltdown, when someone grabbed her arm and whirled her around. She knew who it was before she turned, of course. And though her throat was already far too tight, her heart jerked hard at the sight of Reilly standing there, a little out of breath, his eyes unreadable, his mouth closed in a firm, unhappy line.

When he saw her face, he made a rough sound of regret and brought his other hand up to take her other arm, bringing her close. "You're crying."

"A little," she admitted, and tried to step back from the body she'd grown to love so much.

He held tight. "Don't go."

And her heart broke all the more. "I have to," she said.

"I don't understand," he said. He looked so confused. "Make me understand."

"It's simple, really. Eddie—"

"This isn't about work. I don't give a shit about work. What I do give a shit about is that you're not just walking away from my office, you're walking away from me, aren't you?"

"Actually, it has nothing to do with you." She blinked and another tear fell. *No more,* she promised herself. Not a one. "Remember when I told you I signed up with Eddie for the adventure?"

"Yes."

"His ad promised one." She gave him a watery smile. "It appealed to me because I've lived...well, let's just say conservatively. Part of it is my family and their assumption I can't do anything on my own, but part of it is just me falling into that trap, you know?" But he wouldn't know because Reilly was and always had been his own man. He'd never run his life by the dictates of anyone else. "I wanted more," she said. "And Eddie promised it."

"Well, I'd say you got more than you bargained for on that score," he said softly and skimmed a thumb over her throat.

"I did." So much more. She'd fallen in love. "But now he's offered me this job in the Greek Islands, on a yacht—"

"For how long?"

"It's not that big of a deal, I'll just be doing the books, and—"

"How long?"

"Three months," she replied. She held her breath. "A perfect adventure, don't you think?"

He stared at her for a long moment during which she waited for him to say that a better adventure would be for her to stay, to be with him.

Instead, he slowly nodded. He took his hands from her and slid them into his pockets. "I hope it's everything you wanted."

No, everything she ever wanted was right here in front of her. But sometimes people had to go for their second choices. "Thank you."

"When do you leave?"

"Monday."

"That's still several days away."

No doubt, he was thinking they could have several more wild nights together, nights that would be the most heaven-sent she'd ever had. She was quite certain he'd see to it—the earthy, sensual, incredibly passionate man was made for such nights.

But then Monday would come and it would be even harder to walk away. She opened her car door. Slid into the driver's seat.

And wondered why she was still waiting for him to stop her.

He wasn't going to do that. He wasn't going to say he wanted those few nights they had left. That he'd love to see her when she got back.

In fact, he said nothing.

She put on her seat belt, put the key in the ignition and tried to convince herself she'd done the right thing.

A sleek red BMW convertible pulled up beside her and honked. Eddie, of course. He took down his sunglasses and winked at her over the top of them. Then, with an ease that made him seem twenty-nine instead of forty-nine, he hopped over the door of his car and walked toward Cheri, who was coming out of the building.

Still standing next to her car, his hands in his pockets, Reilly took this in with a muttered oath beneath his breath.

Tessa appreciated the sentiment. She always enjoyed both Eddie's and Cheri's company, but their timing couldn't have been worse. She just wanted to drive away. She wanted to go home and lick her wounds with a gallon of ice cream and maybe some Ding Dongs as well. She had an emergency stash in the freezer.

Eddie took Cheri's hand and turned to Reilly. "I fired Cheri this morning," he said.

Reilly shook his head and looked at Cheri. "He fired you? But...I thought you worked for me."

"You poor confused thing." Cheri hugged him then pulled back. "Remember when I told you I was going to start dating him because he was cute?"

"You said I was cute?" Eddie said, grinning. "I was thinking handsome and magnificent, but I can live with cute."

"Shh," Cheri said gently to him and turned back to Reilly. "Actually, I'm going to marry him. I'm going to make it official."

Reilly looked like a feather could knock him over. "Make what official?" he asked.

"The fact that I'm sleeping with him, of course."

Cheri laughed. "Be happy for me, honey. Can you do that?"

"Of course he can do that," Eddie said, breaking in. "Right, son?"

"And what makes you think she's not going to dump you again?" Reilly asked him.

Eddie clasped him on the shoulder. "Son, sometimes you just have to take a risk and go with your heart."

Reilly looked at Tessa with such intensity and blazing emotion in his light eyes that it took her breath away.

"There's nothing like a good risk to jump-start your heart," Eddie ruffled his own dark hair, barely speckled at the temples. "It causes gray hairs, of course, but that's what beauticians are for."

Tessa held her breath. It didn't take a rocket scientist to see what Reilly's father was trying to tell him. Take a risk. Love again. Feel.

Live.

But was he hearing it? She searched his inscrutable expression and didn't have a clue.

"Beat it," Reilly suddenly said to his parents, his eyes still on Tessa.

"Sure." Eddie turned to Cheri. "Let's go make out."

Reilly winced. "What in our history together suggests to you that I'd want to hear that?"

Cheri laughed and reached for Eddie. "You know what? *Let's.* I think the kid wants to be alone."

"Nothing wrong with that," Eddie said. He helped

Cheri into the convertible, winked once more at Tessa and then drove off.

"They were wrong," Reilly said. "I don't want to be alone." He reached into her car and took her keys out of the ignition. "I should warn you, I'm moody."

She lifted a brow.

"I'm also...grumpy sometimes."

"Tell me something I don't know," she said cautiously, and he nodded.

"I will. But first..."

She watched him pocket her keys and wondered what he was up to.

"Tell me that you'll think of me every day of those three months of your adventure," he said. "That it's killing you to walk away."

She closed her eyes, then opened them again and met his. "Of course it's hard to walk away. We've slept together. We made love in your bathroom," she said, her voice quivering a little and he grimaced.

"I know," he said. "God, I know. You don't take that lightly and—"

"Lightly?" She said, laughing and shook her head. "You want to know what I don't take lightly? Falling in love with you, you idiot."

He stared at her. Then he opened the car door and hauled her out. Lifted her up to her toes to look her in the eye. Nose to nose he said, "Then why the hell are you leaving?"

"Because..." She lifted her hands to his face, which

she lovingly cupped. "I didn't want to be the only one in love."

"Now who's the idiot?" He set her down gently, wrapped his arms around her. "I do love you. I love you so much you're driving me right out of my living mind."

It was her turn to stare at him, speechless. Then she both laughed and cried and took one of her hands off his face so she could smack his shoulder. "You might have said so."

"I did," he said, and put his forehead to hers. "In every kiss, in every look and every touch."

"And you were going to let me walk away?"

"I wouldn't have held you back, not from your adventure."

"You love me that much?"

"Look, I've screwed up at love before. I've gone the opposite route and closed myself off, and screwed that up, too. Neither worked for me, but then you came along—"

She made a soft noise of emotion, of hope and joy, and he hugged her. "I know how to put numbers together," he said in her ear. "I know how to get them to make sense. I know how to do a lot of things, but loving you...I don't have a clue." He pulled back to see her face. "All I know is that your smile makes my day and that when I'm with you, everything seems right."

"Oh, Reilly," she sighed, devouring his mouth. Just plastered herself against him, sank her fingers into his hair and kissed him desperately, hungrily. She kissed him with everything she had, everything she wanted to give him.

"So you're staying," he finally said, his voice unsteady and missing its usual easy confidence.

Tessa buried her face in his throat, inhaling him, just breathing him in. "I don't know...that was a heck of a job offer from Eddie. I mean, the Greek Islands? Think of the experience."

He tightened his hands on her. "I can offer a chance for experience, too."

"Really?" she asked. She cocked her head. "What do you have in mind?"

He whispered in her ear, low, raw, earthy suggestions, things no one had ever whispered to her before. Excited, aroused and her heart overflowing, she nodded. "Sounds like quite an opportunity."

"Oh, yes," he agreed and put her back into the car, this time on the passenger side. He got in behind the wheel. "In fact, there's no need to wait, we can start—"

"Now?"

"*Now*." He drove her to his house.

"But work—"

"Forget work. I gave Marge the day off to go do something special, something she'd never done before," he said. "I told her I was going to do the same," he said, smiling at her, a smile full of so much love she felt her eyes well up again.

And his quickly faded. "What's the matter?"

"I always wanted to fall in love with a man who'd show me his feelings," she said slowly. "A man who was warm and compassionate and soft—"

"Wait a minute." He turned off the engine, then led her inside. Once there, he took her hand and led her to his bedroom. "Warm and compassionate, no problem. Or at least I can try.... But that being *soft* thing—"

She laughed.

He pressed against her, so far from soft that her laugh turned into a little gasp.

"You think this condition is amusing?"

"Only because..." She paused and looked at his bed.

"Because..." he said helpfully, drawing her to his mattress, where he started in on her buttons.

"Because I know how to relieve the condition," she said, assuring him and started on his buttons, too. "We've finally got it right. We've finally made it to a bed."

"Finally." He held her off, the playfulness gone. "Right place, right time, right woman. It's all just right. You're everything to me," he said softly. *"Everything."*

She reached for him, half-undressed, holding him close, so close that she could feel his heart beating against hers, could feel the two different patterns merge, become one. And she sighed as her world became complete.

Epilogue

Fifteen months later

THE GREEK ISLANDS were lovely this time of year. Tessa let out a languid sigh and figured she was the luckiest woman on earth.

She was in her bathing suit, lying on her back, staring up at an azure summer sky so amazing it took her breath away. Beneath her, the yacht rocked gently in the breeze, the water lapping at the sides with a pleasant, hypnotic sound.

"Mrs. Ledger?"

That brought a smile to her face, though she didn't turn toward the male voice. "Yes?"

"I've brought you your sunscreen. Turn over and I'll rub it on you."

With a naughty smile, she turned onto her belly and wriggled a little to get comfortable on her towel—and to show off her backside.

She gasped when the tie of her bikini top was tugged free, then set to her sides. Then the cold lotion was squirted on the small of her back, making her gasp again.

"Mmm, nice," he breathed into her ear. His hands

touched her, slid over her muscles and warm skin in a way that made her moan, without the strap of her top across her back to encumber him in any way. Up and down, then to the backs of her legs, even dipping into her bikini bottoms enough to have her wriggling some more.

"Does your husband know what I do to you?" he whispered, his fingers getting quite wicked, making her lose her train of thought.

Hmm. To even the score, she flipped over and exposed her bare breasts. She looked up into Reilly's face. "He knows," she said, feeling smug at the glossy look in his eyes as he devoured the sight of her.

He cupped her breasts, gently stroking her nipples, and it was her turn to give him a glassy-eyed look. "Husband," she managed to say. "I like that word."

"Do you?" He leaned in and kissed her mouth softly, settling one big hand on her belly.

"You know what word I like even more?" she asked.

"What?" He gave her the indulgent smile of a man on his honeymoon, a man who knew he was about to get very lucky for the third time that day.

"Daddy," she whispered. "I like the word daddy." She watched as he went very still.

His eyes cut to the hand he held on her still-flat belly, his fingers tightening a little as his eyes went hot with that wild emotion called love.

"Remember on your desk last month?" she asked softly. "When the condom broke—"

"I remember."

"Well, funny thing about broken condoms..."

His eyes cut to hers. "Are you saying—"

"Would you mind a whole lot?" she asked, holding her breath.

"Mind a whole lot?" he repeated and closed his eyes. When he opened them, they were bright and just a little damp. His voice broke, his breath hitched. "Minding isn't quite the right word."

Her own breath hitched, too. "What is?"

"Ecstatic," he said fervently. "Blown away. Overcome." He spread his fingers wide on her stomach, his expression pure love and protectiveness. Then he bent his head and kissed her right below her belly button. "Another generation..." He let out a breath.

"Terrified?"

"Only slightly," he admitted, then scooped her up in his arms, against his chest. "I'm crazy in love with you, Tess."

"I know." Her joy complete, she sighed with pleasure. "Let's go inside, back to our stateroom. You can show me just how much..."

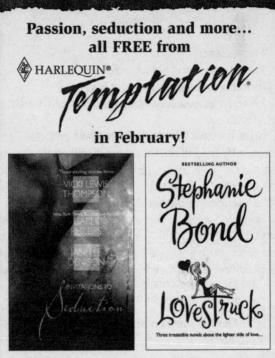

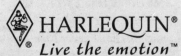